About the author

I currently live in upstate New York surrounded by my husband, kids, and grandkids. I have traveled extensively thanks to being part of a military family. I have many interests such as hiking, writing, photography, and traveling. I am a teacher as well as a writer and I love every minute of both!

I am working on another novel and I really enjoy connecting with my readers.

FINDING ME

Connie Spanhake

FINDING ME

Vanguard Press

VANGUARD PAPERBACK

A CIP catalogue record for this title is
available from the British Library.

ISBN 978 1 784654 66 5

Vanguard Press is an imprint of
Pegasus Elliot MacKenzie Publishers Ltd.
www.pegasuspublishers.com

First Published in 2018

Vanguard Press
Sheraton House, Castle Park
Cambridge England

Printed & Bound in Great Britain

Acknowledgments

I would like to acknowledge a few people without whom this never would have been possible. I would like to say a huge thank you to my husband, Roy Spanhake, for always supporting and encouraging me. My read behinds, Joyce and Samuel Dean, Cheri Dean, Anastasia Spanhake, Shaila Carr, and Eileen Johnson who gave great advice even when they were sure that I wouldn't like what they were going to say. I would like to thank Cathy Wade for her guidance. I would also like to thank Vanguard Press, an imprint of Pegasus Elliot Mackenzie, for publishing this book and bringing these characters to life.

Dedication

For those who stand beside us in good times and in bad

Prologue

Sirens! The sound was deafening. Jenna tried to open her eyes to see what was happening, but they refused to open. It was as if they were shielding her from something horrific.

Somewhere off to her left she heard a man yelling and someone else groaning in pain. What's going on? She tried to move but her body wouldn't cooperate.

"Over here!" a man yelled. "There's another one over here!"

Another what? Or who? Slowly, Jenna began to remember. The squealing tires, the broken glass, the car careening out of control and then metal clashing with pavement as it rolled and rolled and rolled.

She wanted to move. She tried to yell. There were sirens again but this time they were growing fainter in the distance. Are they leaving? Why? *I'm still here*! Jenna tried to make some kind of sound, something, *anything*, to get their attention. The wet, muddy ground permeated her senses. She felt trapped and unable to move. The cool rain pelted her skin, trickling off her body, and combined with the soil underneath her. It was so cold. This must be what death feels like. Still no one came, and everything slowly began to turn quiet except for the rain falling from the sky. It was so cold, she felt so tired, and why doesn't anyone come? Sleep began to overpower her body. She tried to fight it but now it doesn't seem to matter. It doesn't even hurt any more.

"I've got one," someone shouted. "The pulse is faint but it's there. Stay with me, young lady. You're going to be okay." Jenna felt her body being lifted off of the cold, dank ground. Someone was sliding an oxygen mask over her face.

She heard the buzzing of a scanner then a male voice. "A young female, twenty-one years of age, unresponsive, ETA is 7 minutes."

Are they talking about me?

"Just stay with me we're almost there," ordered a deep commanding voice off to the left of her. The blaring siren was suddenly quiet, and the ambulance came to a stop. Jenna heard doors flying open. Voices were yelling vital information such as BP and lacerations. The wheels underneath her were moving faster and the sound of electronic doors quickly sliding open as chaos continued to ensue all around. There were people everywhere sticking, poking, and prodding. Jenna wanted to sit up and scream STOP but she couldn't move, couldn't talk. She felt herself falling back into darkness. It was quiet and calm. Why couldn't she just be left alone?

A sharp pain shot through Jenna's leg and she immediately started to groan. She forced her eyes open but quickly closed them against the shock of the harsh light shining in from the window. Jenna opened them again, this time a little more cautiously, and peered at a young nurse writing something on her chart. The nurse quickly looked up and walked towards her and pushed a button on her IV. Jenna hoped it was something to dull the excruciating pain that had taken over her body.

"You're awake." The nurse smiled brightly. "Your parents are in the waiting room and are eager to see you."

Jenna, still groggy, started to panic, "Where am I?"

The young nurse remained calm. "You are at St. John's Hospital."

Three quick knocks rapped on the door and a man wearing a white hospital lab coat and round rimmed glasses entered the room. His blue eyes studied her as he smiled. "Hi Jenna, I'm Dr. Andrews. You're looking much better than when I first saw you." He walked over to her bed and picked up her chart and read it over.

He put the chart down and took out a small, thin light. "This may be a little bright but please just bear with me. Look up," he ordered. "Now look to the side." Jenna did as he asked. "Can you tell me your name?" he asked.

"Jenna Lewis," she replied.

"Very good," he replied. "Do you know the date?" he asked.

Jenna thought for a minute. "March twenty-fifth, 2016." The doctor clicked off the light and slipped it into his pocket as he continued his examination by pushing and prodding every aching area on her body.

He continued talking while he examined the sutures on her leg. “You’re close. That was the day of your accident. Today is March twenty-seventh, 2016.” Jenna looked shocked. “Don’t be concerned,” said Dr. Andrews. “It’s perfectly normal. You suffered a severe trauma and you have been sedated for the last couple of days to allow time for your body to heal. It’s understandable that you aren’t sure what day it is.”

When he finished he took off his gloves and said, “You are a very lucky young lady. I know you have a few questions and I promise I will answer each one, but for the time being it’s extremely important that you just rest. I’ll tell your parents that you’re awake and I’ll come back to check on you in a little while.”

The nurse followed Dr. Andrews out through the door and Jenna looked around the sterile room. The smell of antiseptic permeated the room and the machines beeping behind her were a constant reminder of how lucky she had been. Jenna shakily tried to shift her body into a sitting position. Sharp pains shot through her head and the room began to spin along with a wave of nausea bubbling up from within her.

Jenna’s parents entered the room just as she exclaimed, “I’m going to be sick!” Her mom raced to the table and grabbed a metal container and held it under Jenna’s face as she began to vomit. Her body convulsed as she continued to dry heave. She could feel beads of sweat forming on her forehead. It felt like a lifetime before she finally stopped and could breathe again. She was afraid to move but her mom gently guided her back into a sitting position. Jenna felt exhausted and helpless as her mother wet a washcloth and placed it on her forehead. She wanted to ask what happened. She had so many questions but her eyes betrayed her and closed as she quietly drifted away into a drug induced sleep.

Jenna didn't know how long she had been asleep, but she could hear her parents whispering in hushed tones to one another. Her father's voice sounded angry. "I told you those girls were nothing but trouble!"

She could hear her mom sobbing. "I'm sure there's a perfectly good explanation for this Charles. Let's give her a chance to explain."

Explain? Explain what? Jenna tried to open her eyes, but they wouldn't cooperate. She continued to lie still in her bed and listened.

Her dad's shoes squeaked a little as he paced back and forth. "Drugs and alcohol? We raised her better than this!"

What are they talking about? Jenna tried once again to open her eyes and this time they slowly fluttered open.

Her mom instantly raced to Jenna's side. "Oh, Jenna you're awake! How are you feeling darling? Do you want me to call the doctor?"

Jenna tried to lick her lips, but her mouth was dry and her lips felt cracked. Her mom quickly poured a glass of water and slid a straw into the cup. She moved the straw towards Jenna's mouth and helped her to take a cautious sip. It tasted so cool and refreshing. Jenna reached for the glass with shaky hands, took another sip, leaned back onto her pillow, and closed her eyes.

Her mom gently ran her fingers through Jenna's hair pushing it back. In a raspy voice Jenna asked, "What happened?"

Jenna's mom choked back a sob as she said, "You've suffered some head trauma and have a concussion. Your leg is broken in two places and you had to have pins put in..."

Jenna interrupted her, "No, Mom, I mean what happened?"

The door suddenly swung open as Dr. Andrews and a police officer stepped inside. The doctor looked grim as he stood in the background. The police officer walked over to Jenna and began to rattle off what seemed to be a long-rehearsed speech. "Jenna Lewis, you are hereby under arrest for operating a vehicle under the influence of drugs and alcohol and of second degree manslaughter in the death of Cara Donnelly. You have the right to remain silent. Anything you say and do can and will be used against you in a court of law. You have a right to an attorney. If you cannot afford an attorney, one will be appointed to you. Do you understand these rights as they have been read to you?"

Jenna looked over at her mom. "WHAT HAPPENED?" she screamed. Her mom sat silently with tears streaming down her face. Her dad looked at her with disgust and walked out the door without looking back.

"Jenna," repeated the officer. "Do you understand these rights as they have been read to you?"

"Yes," she whispers.

Chapter 1
Jenna
August 21, 2014

Jenna walked into her psychology class and looked for a seat towards the back of the room. It was her first day of class at McClellan University and she was having a difficult time calming her nerves. She looked around the room and noted that it was typical of any other classroom she sat in during high school. There were stark white walls contrasting with green tile floors and empty desks placed in rows facing a newly polished white board. Eventually, other students began to trickle in and the murmur of voices slowly began to bring the room to life. A small group of students were softly talking in the far corner of the room while other students were content to sit quietly and text on their phone. Jenna liked the anonymity of being in a place where no one knew her.

The professor walked in at precisely eleven. She was tall and looked to be in her early fifties. She had thick red hair pulled up into a tight bun and was dressed in a no nonsense black pantsuit. She placed her matching black briefcase on top of her desk, clicked it open, and pulled out a thick stack of papers.

She slipped on her glasses, stepped up to the podium, and cleared her throat. The room began to grow silent as students put away their phones and directed their attention towards the front of the room.

"This is Psychology 101 and I am Professor Kenton. I am handing out this semester's syllabus. Please take one and pass it on." Professor Kenton's heels clicked across the floor as she walked over to a girl sitting in the front row and handed the papers to her. The girl confidently took a syllabus off the top of the stack and placed it on her desk. She pasted a smile on her face as she handed the stack to a nervous looking young man sitting next to her. The girl had shoulder length blond hair pulled back into a ponytail. She wore a pair of black leggings with a long thick green sweater. She had her notebook out ready to take notes and was currently reading over the syllabus highlighting important due dates.

***

"Here you go," a girl said sitting beside me. I smiled and reached for the last syllabus.

"Thanks," I said. *Focus Jenna,* I remind myself. Class hasn't even started yet and I'm already spacing out. I push back my long brown hair and tuck it behind my ear. I was going to cut it short as I began this new chapter in my life, but at the last minute I chickened out. That's me, Jenna, a girl who can't seem to make up her mind. Ever.

Professor Kenton walked over and perched herself on the corner of her desk. "Since we will be working with one another this semester I would like to begin by everyone introducing themselves."

I groaned. I guess college isn't all that different than high school after all. I hated when instructors did this! No one cares what anyone's major is and I really, really, hate to be the center of attention even if it is for only thirty seconds. I tried listening and focusing my attention.

Professor Kenton looked around the room until her eyes rested on the blond girl who sat in the front row. "Why don't we start with you," the professor said smiling.

The girl stood up and smiled as she faced everyone. "My name is Cara and I am a nursing major. I come from a small town and I enjoy hiking, working out, and I am a vegetarian." She sat back down.

The instructor looked down at the roster and said, "Jenna?"

I stood up and cleared my throat. "My name is Jenna and I am a law major. I love junk food, sleeping in, and I am a carnivore." I looked over at Cara and saw her roll her eyes. I shot her a victorious smile and sat down.

As the next person stood up to introduce themselves I thought about how I described myself. Okay, so I may be a bit of a rebel and if my parents would have described me it would have been different. Their rendition would have been something like she's a troublemaker, party girl, liar, and lazy. I'm not going to lie and say those things aren't true. I have had a history of shoplifting. People would ask me, 'Why did you do it?' and I really don't have much of an answer except that there's a thrill in not getting caught, besides I didn't lift expensive items just little shit, but to this day I've never heard the end of it. As for being a party girl who doesn't like going to a good party?

I thought back to the ultimatum I was given the day after I graduated. I had bounced down the stairs and walked into the kitchen. I sat down at the table, pouring myself a glass of orange juice, relishing in my new-found freedom. My mom was standing at the stove frying bacon and my dad, like every morning before, was reviewing the latest stock prices. I still cringe when I think of how my dad folded his newspaper and cleared his throat. He looked first at Mom and then zeroed in on me and said, "Jenna, now that you've graduated what are your plans?"

I laughed and said, "What do you mean what are my plans? Right now, it looks like breakfast."

Mom interrupted, "Charles, maybe this isn't the time."

Dad glared at Mom and then at me. "This is the perfect time. I'm just going to come right out and say it. Jenna, you have a choice. You can either apply to a college and pray they will accept you or move out and live on your own. It's time for you to grow up."

I looked from one to the other, "You've got to be kidding!"

Mom didn't say a word, but Dad continued, "We're serious Jenna. We are no longer going to clean up your messes or call in favors so that you won't be arrested. We're tired of waiting up for you and wondering if you were in an accident or worse. You have a month to figure it out." Dad calmly laid his paper down on the table, kissed Mom on the cheek, and left for work.

I looked over at Mom. "You're just going to let him kick me out like that?"

Mom walked over to me and put her hand on my shoulder. "Oh honey," she said. "I know it's hard but it's time for you to take responsibility for yourself."

I shrugged my arm away from her touch and angrily pushed back my chair. "Fine, I don't need you. I don't need him. And I don't need a month to decide!" I grabbed my purse and keys and slammed the door behind me.

I tried to refocus my attention back to the instructor as she went over the syllabus. It wasn't working. I remember peeling out of the driveway and racing down my street. I had planned on staying with my best friend, Casey, but she wasn't home, and her parents said they'd love to help but there just wasn't room. They lived in a huge four-bedroom house and there were only three of them. Where was there not enough room? I went to Jason's next. We had a "friends with benefits" arrangement, and he had his own place. I knocked quickly and then walked in before he had a chance to answer. I heard noises coming from the bedroom. I quietly walked down the hallway and opened the door.

Apparently, he had "other" friends with benefits, and that friend happened to be Casey. I pushed the door open farther and yelled, "You have got to be kidding!"

Casey jumped out of bed and rapidly began throwing on her clothes. "It's not what it seems, Jenna. Let me explain."

Jason sat up in bed and frowned. "I don't need girl drama. Both of you get the hell out of my house."

I lost it. He hadn't seen drama yet. I walked over to his side of the bed and smiled, then made a fist with my hand and punched him right in the groin. He was doubled over as Casey stood speechless.

I walked over towards Casey, my hands still clenched. Casey backed up and braced herself for the punch she knew was coming. Instead, I stopped and glared at her the silence growing heavier between us.

Casey murmured, "I'm sorry. It just happened." I stared at her in disbelief and slowly turned to leave slamming the door behind me. I never looked back.

Which is how I found myself here at McClellan University. I figured either way my parents would pay. I made sure my parents were paying for my tuition, my room and board, and I figured that although I planned to drop out the first chance I got I might as well major in law so I know how to get myself out of situations. Dad made it perfectly clear I was on my own.

I was startled back into the present when there were loud sounds of chairs being slid back and people gathering their things. I looked down at my syllabus and noticed I did not write one single note. I crammed it into my already too full backpack, stood up, and tried not to look like a confused idiot as I walked out the door. I turned left and hoped I was going the right way as I followed the masses down the hallway that led to a set of doors. Thankfully, I pushed open the doors and walked outside into the bright sunlight.

***

Cara was standing off to the side of the building smoking a cigarette. Jenna laughed and shook her head when she saw her.

"What?" Cara demanded.

"I did NOT expect that," Jenna chuckled, pointing to Cara's cigarette.

Cara looked down at her cigarette and smiled. "Yeah, I guess you're right. I'm a health junkie with a bad habit. That's me," Cara said, taking a drag of her cigarette and then looking back at Jenna. "Do you want one?" Cara asked.

Jenna tried to look shocked. "Are you crazy? Those things will kill you!"

Cara laughed, and Jenna looked down at her watch. "I am starving though, and I have an hour before my next class. Do you want to grab some lunch?"

"Sure," Cara replied snuffing out her cigarette. The two girls started walking toward the dining hall.

"Are all first day classes this boring?" Jenna asked.

"Yep," replied Cara putting her sunglasses over her eyes.

The lobby was crowded when they walked through the door. Jenna scanned the crowd and said, "I'll grab us a table while you grab lunch."

Cara nodded and walked toward the salad bar. Jenna watched her pick through the vegetables selecting only the freshest ingredients. Jenna shook her head and rolled her eyes. *It figures that the only friend I have is the opposite of me.*

Cara walked over to the table with her plate and a bottle of water. Jenna looked at her and shook her head. Cara smiled smugly at Jenna who turned and walked straight towards the hamburger stand. There was nothing better than fried food. She ordered a burger with cheese fries and grabbed a bottle of soda. As she waited for her order she noticed that two other girls had joined Cara. *Great,* she thought, feeling her anxiety level rising. *Well, gotta make friends sometime, I guess.*

"That'll be $6.50," the cashier announced.

Jenna pulled out her dining card and handed it to the cashier who quickly scanned it and handed it back already speaking to the next person in line. She picked up her food and pasted on a smile as she turned around and saw Cara waving from their table. Jenna balanced her burger and fries in one hand and her drink in the other as she carefully began to weave her way towards the table.

The two strangers looked up at Jenna as one of them said, "I hope you don't mind us sitting here but there are no other seats."

"No problem. I'm Jenna by the way." She sat down not quite sure what to say. She felt so out of her league here. She took a bite of her burger and sipped her drink. She tried to look confident and unnerved. She studied the girl sitting across from her. Allie was her name. She was rambling on about being an interior designer and she definitely looked like the artsy type. She was dressed in a long flowing skirt with colorful swirls along with a green halter top. She had huge gold hoop earrings peering out from her tri-colored curly hair that was pulled back in a headband and she had a variety of charm bracelets dangling from her wrist. She seemed very relaxed and talked as though she had known us forever.

Jenna remained quiet trying not to draw attention to herself, but Allie locked her big brown eyes onto her and asked, "So how do you like your classes so far?"

Jenna took a sip of her drink and replied, "They seem okay. I think the Psychology course is going to be a lot of work and I'm a little worried about math."

Allie exclaimed, "You're in luck! I've already taken the Psychology course, so I can help you, and my friend Kym is a business major. If you have any questions about math, then she's your go to girl."

In hearing her name Kym turned to look at us. "What are you volunteering me for Allie?"

Allie smiled and said, "I was just explaining to Jenna that you're a math genius."

Kym nodded, checked her watch, and said, "Speaking of classes I've gotta go, my next class is in five minutes and I don't want to be late."

Allie said, "I should be going too." She stood up and lugged her bag up over her shoulders. Then she leaned over and picked up a fry that was oozing with cheese. She popped it in her mouth and rolled her eyes in elated satisfaction. "Let's all meet up later," Allie suggested as she sauntered out of the overcrowded dining hall without looking back.

Chapter 2
Cara

I couldn't wait to get out of Psychology class. All of those first-year students have so much to learn. I know I should be more patient, but this is my last year of college and I have put this class off until near the end of my studies. I figured that being a nurse will require more than just medical skills and having some background in psychology will help my career. It'll probably help me too since I am definitely a Type A personality.

I pull out my phone and look down at the screen. I have a text message waiting. I smile already knowing who it's from.

Trent: I Love You

Cara: I Love you too xoxoxo

Trent: How's your class?

Cara: Okay. I'll be glad when classes are over and we are together again. I miss you.

Trent: Miss you too babe

I drop my phone in my purse and look around me as other students saunter past heading to their next class or back to their dorm. I'm excited to finally move into this phase of my life. It's been a long time coming. I look down at the ring Trent put on my finger before we both left for college and smile. We've been dating for three years and plan on spending the rest of our lives together.

I stand off to the side of the building and pull out a cigarette, light up, and take a long drag. It helps to calm my nerves and relaxes me. When people discover I smoke AND I'm a nursing student I always have to explain myself. If people only knew the stress I'm under maybe they'd let up. They would be shocked if they knew just how many doctors and nurses smoke.

I begin walking across campus to my next class, Nursing: Transition to Professional Practice. The trees are starting to change color from greens to bright oranges and yellows. I love the sights and smells of fall. It's one of my favorite seasons. I look up at the old red brick building and see the plaque above the door, Keyser Hall. I walk into the building and down the newly waxed hallway. I step into the room and sit at the first desk in the first row. I am a creature of habit and enjoy the structure of the first day of classes. It's the same old routine. Sit in class. Introduce yourself. Review the syllabus and go over expectations. I am glad this is the last class for the day. I am exhausted.

I look down at my watch and see that it is five thirty. I only have fifteen minutes left. I finish taking notes and let out a sigh of relief when the day is finally over. I slide the syllabus into my folder and slip it into my already full backpack. When I get home, I'll start on my first assignment. I've always been organized and always a step ahead. I never run late, and I've never turned in anything less than my best. That explains my 3.9 GPA.

I walk back to my dorm and let myself in. My roommate, Sasha, seems nice enough but she is flighty and always losing things. Last night it was her car keys that had us looking for hours, only for her to find them in the bottom of her purse which she swore she had already checked five times before. Things like this usually drive me crazy so I spend most of my time at the library or, if it's a weekend, I drive up and stay with Trent.

I looked around our small living/dining combo and see that Sasha has made herself dinner and left all the dirty dishes piled up on the counter, along with the television blaring. I roll my eyes and turn off the television. I don't know which is worse when Sasha is here with her cackling friends or when she's gone leaving a huge mess in her wake. I make a quick left into the bedroom and shut myself in. This is the only way I can cope otherwise I'll start cleaning and that will take up most of my night.

I sit on my bed and begin to pull out each syllabus and put them in a colored folder. I have a color coordinated notebook for each class as well. I pull out my note cards and start writing notes from my Psychology class.

The front door slams as Sasha yells, "Cara, girl, are you here?"

I roll my eyes wishing I could just disappear. Sasha begins talking to someone and quickly raps three times on my door and swings my door open before I have a chance to say anything. Sasha comes bounding into my room along with her usual group of friends. They were hysterically laughing and hooting as Sasha regaled how some guy had hit on her today. It was impossible to concentrate. I smile and listen to my new roommate wondering how I'm ever going to survive the semester living with her.

"Cara, you gotta check out that new professor, Mr. Stark. He is a fine lookin' man."

I laugh, shake my head, and walk out of the room to grab a water bottle. I hear Sasha and her friends debating which professor is better looking.

I grab my coat and my nursing manual and step outside. I take a deep breath in the brisk night air and relish the peace and quiet. I don't know how I'm going to survive Sasha for a whole year. I walk over to the dining hall and order a latte. I sip it at the same table I had been sitting at during lunch. I open up my nursing book and begin to read the first chapter.

"Hey," Jenna said in surprise. "Great minds think alike."

I look up and laugh. Jenna is holding a latte in her left hand and her Psychology book in her right. I knew then that we were going to be friends.

She sits down and motions towards my book. "Are you just starting your program?" Jenna asks.

I smile. "No, actually I'm almost finished. I start my rotations at Brixton Hospital next semester."

Jenna smiled ruefully. "I'm so jealous."

"No, you aren't. You are just discovering the wonders of being on your own and all the fun things that college has to offer," I finish sarcastically.

Jenna shook her head and laughed, "Being on my own definitely, but college being fun I have yet to see."

"Give it time," I said.

We both sit at the table and open our books. I take notes diligently as Jenna reads her book and sips on her latte. I like that. I hate girls who think they have to constantly talk and can't stand silence. The dining hall slowly becomes sparse as each hour passes. Eventually, my eyes begin to burn and I start to yawn. I look at my watch and see that it is eleven thirty. I glance over at Jenna and notice that she has fallen asleep reading. One thing that all college students can agree on is that textbooks are not riveting.

I close my book and gently shake Jenna's shoulder. She jumps and looks up glassy eyed. She runs a hand over her face and says, "God, I hope I wasn't drooling."

I burst out laughing. "Don't worry, you weren't drooling but you were snoring."

"I was not!" Jenna replies in horror.

I smile. "I'll never tell." We both laugh and gather our things.

As we walk outside in the cool night air Jenna asks, "Are you going back to your dorm?"

I groan. "Unfortunately, yes."

"What's so unfortunate about it?" Jenna asked.

"My roommate," I reply. "She's nice and all but she doesn't clean up after herself and she has a bunch of friends over. It's impossible to study and I doubt I'll get much sleep tonight."

"Do you want to stay at my place?" Jenna asks. "I have a roommate, but I've never met her. She's always gone. You can sleep on the couch."

I yawn again and look over at my dorm building. I can see the lights from my room still shining bright. Either the girls are still on a roll or Sasha forgot to turn off the light. Either way it didn't take me long to decide. "Thanks, I'll take you up on your offer." We walk towards her dorm room on the other side of the campus. "What made you choose law as your major?" I ask, pulling my jacket tighter around me.

Jenna laughed. "You wouldn't believe me if I told you."

Now she really had me curious. "Give me a try."

Jenna shrugged and said, "Okay. My parents gave me an ultimatum to either go to college or move out of the house. My plan was to move out but that didn't pan out. In the past I had gotten into a few scrapes with the law. I figured pursuing a law degree would really make them pay up until I drop out which I'm planning to do once I can afford to. Until then I thought that it wouldn't hurt to know my rights."

"Wow," I said. "That is not what I was expecting. I thought it would be because you believed in justice and wanted to make the world a better place."

Jenna thought for a minute and said, "Well, I do believe in justice and making the world a better place although probably not as a lawyer, but who knows maybe I'll change my mind."

We reach Jenna's dorm and she unlocks the door. I look around and I am relieved to see that her place is orderly and not in total disarray like my place.

Jenna grabbed an extra blanket and pillow and set it on the couch. She looks at me. "What made you decide to be a nurse?"

I smile sadly. "I was very close to my grandmother. She always took care of me when my mom was at work because my dad was never around. I really can't recall a day I wasn't with her. One day my grandmother started feeling ill and went to lie down. Everyone thought it was a virus and that she just needed to get some rest. Unfortunately, instead of getting better she continued to get worse. We took her to see her doctor who ran some routine tests. A few days later he called and said that he had made her an appointment to get further testing done at the hospital. In the end we discovered that my grandmother had stage three cancer. Needless to say, we were all shocked. My mom still had to work to pay the bills and by then I was old enough to take care of my grandmother. I would drive her to the hospital where she would go through chemotherapy and radiation. I stayed with her when she was sick and hurting. I was the only one there holding her hand when she passed away. It was awful but from then on, I decided I wanted to help those who were sick and hurting. It's kind of like a tribute to my grandmother."

"That must have been very difficult for you," Jenna said sympathetically.

I shake my head. "It was but I think that's what drives me to be a good nurse, you know? I don't just want to take vitals and make notes on some chart. I want to help people, *really* help. You would be surprised how many people have no one to visit them when they are in the hospital."

Jenna sighed. "I wish I knew what I wanted to do. There's just nothing I feel a strong conviction for."

I shrug and say confidently, "You'll figure it out."

I yawn, and Jenna looks at the clock. "Oh wow, it's late. I have an 8a.m. class and I am not a morning person."

I yawn again and stretch out on the couch under a blanket. "Wake me up before you go so I can get out of your hair," I mumble.

Jenna just shook her head and laughed. "It really doesn't matter. I'm beginning to think my roommate is nonexistent."

I close my eyes. "I'm jealous. I'd love to have my dorm to myself. I wouldn't have to constantly clean up after someone and I'd be able to stay sane."

Jenna laughs. "Yeah but sometimes it's lonely, especially when you don't know anyone."

I smile and reply, "Well, you know someone now."

Jenna smiles warmly. "Yes, and you are welcome here any time." She turns around to go to her room.

"Jenna?"

She stops "Yeah?"

"Thanks," I mumble.

Jenna looked at her friend. "You're welcome."

Chapter 3
Kym

I am so glad this is my last class for the day; Kym thought to herself as she let out a long breath and slid into an empty chair, Finally, I will be done with boring first day introductions and begin working towards my degree. I look at my schedule once again. Trigonometry, six thirty p.m., Professor Snow. I look at the clock once again. It is now six forty-five and still no Professor Snow. This would never happen in China. My parents have raised me to be on time or early. It is a sign of respect.

Professor Snow finally appears, and he looks like his name. He is a short paunchy man with curly white hair and round spectacles sitting atop his nose. He has a short, trimmed beard and walks into the room as though he wasn't late at all.

Professor Snow doesn't say a word but instead turns toward the board and writes Trigonometry 101 in black marker as though we aren't smart enough to know what class this is. Then he turns around and introduces himself. "I'm Professor Snow and this is Trigonometry 101."

I roll my eyes. Not only does he write it but he apparently feels the need to announce it too. He clears his throat and says, "Although you will be working independently for most of this class let's introduce ourselves anyway."

I cringed. No one ever pronounces my last name correctly and this time is no exception. "Kym Signdaykoo," he says, looking around the room.

I slowly stand up. How hard was it to say Syndako? It's pronounced just like it's spelled. "I am Kym Syndako and I have just moved here from China." I see some people look at me with interest while others look at me like I have three heads.

Someone from the back of the room says, "What would possess you to come to McClellan?"

I open my mouth and try to speak but the room erupts in laughter. I begin to feel hot and know my face is turning bright red. I will be so glad when this day is over. I quickly sit back down as Professor Snow proceeds to call on another student.

What would possess me to come to McClellan University? My family, that's what. I hate being so far away from them, but I promised to make them proud. One thing I know for sure is that America is very different from China. Ever since I was little, my parents plan has always been to groom me for America. My father has been tutoring me in my education and later at home for business. I can speak fluent English and do very well with numbers. My family owns a small market where they sell fruits and vegetables and for the past two years I have been their bookkeeper.

Their plan has always been for me to obtain U.S. citizenship and then send for them. Afterward, they will apply for citizenship and my family will live here permanently. During my whole senior year while my friends were going out to parties and dating I was on-line researching everything I had to do to be granted a student visa. Applying for my visa was extremely stressful. Filling out all the paperwork wasn't too awful but going through multiple interviews was nerve wracking and then waiting to see if my citizenship was granted was excruciating. If it were up to me I'd be perfectly content living in China but it's not up to me.

I live in a dorm at McClellan University with my roommate Allie. I haven't known her long, but she seems nice and is very interested in my traditions from China. So, I tell her stories of my homeland. I describe the mountains and rivers that flow through my country. She laughs and says that she had always pictured crowds and tall buildings. I laugh and say that is how I had pictured New York instead of the lavish greenery that surrounds me. Allie tells me that she wants to learn to cook authentic Chinese meals. I tell her I want to learn to cook authentic American meals. She laughs and says America is made up of immigrants, so she isn't quite sure what would constitute an authentic American meal.

Allie is a free spirit. She never seems stressed and everything just comes naturally to her. She is easy to live with and is what people call a minimalist. She doesn't have much in our dorm and says she doesn't need much to survive. Her hair is very different from my own natural black hair. My long straight hair is usually pulled back in a ponytail out of the way. Allie's hair on the other hand is a mixture of brown, white, and purple. Her shoulder length hair is curly and unruly, but she has this way of making it look stylish and natural.

Allie and I have many of the same general education classes. We've already made a pact to help each other through our classes. It's nice knowing that I have someone to rely on. Allie is going to help me through my English Literature class and I am going to help her with her math classes. Although we are still getting to know each other she doesn't know about the expectations my family has placed upon me. I know she would understand if I told her because that's just the way Allie is, but for now I just want to be a normal student in America with a great roommate.

I plop down at the table and pull out my Trigonometry book. Allie walks in and opens the refrigerator, "How was class?" she asks.

I groan. "As horrific as all the others. Why do we have to do introductions? I feel like a robot saying the same thing over and over again."

Allie laughs. "Well, my friend, the horror is over and now the work begins." Allie grabs a glass of water and is dressed in her yoga clothes. "Do you want to do yoga with me?" she asks.

I shake my head no and point to my books.

Allie sighs. "Kym, all work and no play makes for a very dull girl. Have you ever tried yoga?"

"No, but I have a ton of homework to do, Allie."

"You *need* yoga in your life, Kym. It relaxes you and it opens your mind."

I roll my eyes and smile. "Allie, another time okay? Right now, I need to work on Trig. I just want to get off to a good start you know?"

"Oh, Kym, you have so much to learn. I'll let you study but next time you're going to learn the wonders of yoga."

Allie grabbed a grape from the bowl on the counter and popped it in her mouth. "What did you do for fun in China?"

I look at her and said, "To be honest I don't remember. My father is quite strict, and we work a lot."

Allie looks at me surprised and says, "Working is not a bad thing, but you have to enjoy life too. Do you have a boyfriend back home?"

I blush, and Allie immediately picks up on it. "You do have a boyfriend. I want all the details. I can't believe you kept this from me," Allie said teasingly.

I shake my head. "He's not exactly my boyfriend. As I've said, my father is very strict, but we are very attracted to each other and we have been emailing back and forth. He works at my parents' market helping to unload heavy produce, and then when I knew that I was going to leave I trained him to be the bookkeeper."

Allie continued, "Is he cute?"

I feel my cheeks burning. "Yes, he is very handsome. Chao hopes to one day save up enough money to visit me. I miss him very much."

Allie stood and stretched. "I hope I get to meet him one day. He must be very special to have gotten your attention since you seem to always have your nose in a book," she said teasingly.

I laugh at her and shake my head as Allie walks back to her bedroom to do yoga and I go back to working on the problems assigned to me. Numbers are the only thing that seems natural to me in this foreign world.

I look at the clock and see that it's eleven p.m. I yawn and wipe my eyes, which have begun to blur from not taking a break. I stretch trying to work the kinks out of my body and sit back down. Allie stands up from the couch and marches towards me, "Oh no, you're coming with me."

I burst out laughing. "Sorry, Allie, I can't. I'm almost finished."

Instead, she grabs me by the arm and pulls me into her room. "Good, then you can finish in the morning."

I try to protest but it's no use, so I laugh instead as she pulls out a pair of her yoga pants. "Put these on. You'll thank me later."

I walk out of the bathroom dressed in black yoga pants and a pink tank top. Allie begins to lead me in yoga exercises. It feels nice to stretch out all the kinks in my body and I can feel the stress easing out of me. Now I know why Allie makes it a daily ritual. By the time we're finished I'm drenched in sweat but feel amazing.

"You can jump in the shower first," I tell Allie.

"Are you sure?"

"Yes, I have to..."

Allie interrupts. "Please don't say finish your homework."

I laugh. "No, I was going to say that I have to email my parents. They worry about me, so I want to check in."

"Okay," Allie replies. "I'll be quick."

I log onto my computer and see that I have two emails waiting for me. One is from Chao and the other is from my father. I open Chao's first.

My Lovely Kym,

I miss you more as each day passes. I think about your smile and my heart breaks. I hear from your father that you are doing well with your classes. I knew you would. I have some news! I have joined the People's Liberation Army. I know you will not be pleased by my decision but I have nothing to offer you and your father will surely deny my request to be with you. By joining the PLA, I will have money and will gain respect. I'm hoping to save up sooner so that I can visit you and take you on a proper date. I love you, Kym, and miss you terribly. I will not be able to write for a while as I will be away in training. Do not worry, Kym, this is for the best.

Love,

Chao

I sit in stunned silence and reread the email. I feel abandoned and betrayed. Before I left I begged him to not enlist with the PLA. I pleaded with him to stay and work at the market with my parents. I know that eventually they will come to love him as much as I do. In exasperation she opened up the next email from her father.

Dear Kym,

I hope your classes are going well. If you work hard and study you will be successful. We cannot wait to come to America and start our lives anew. You will make us very proud. I love you my daughter.

With Much Love,
Your Father

I sit in front of the computer wishing I could tell my father how much I love Chao and to ask that he encourage Chao to change his mind, but I can't. I feel trapped here and resent being so far away. I wish I could fly home and study there but that would be disappointing to my father so instead I write about my classes and about Allie.

Dear Father,

I have been working very hard with my studies. My roommate is helping me with English Literature and I help her with mathematics. My classes are going well and Allie is a great roommate. I can't wait until you and Mother will be here. I will do what is necessary to please you.

Love,
Kym

"Kym, I'm finished. Your turn," Allie yells from the doorway.

I send my email and log off the computer. I am so homesick. I think of Chao and I miss him so much. My heart breaks knowing I can't talk to him. I think about the regular patrons that visit the market. I think of my mother helping them pick out only the best fruits and vegetables. My father is always talking politics with the local residents. I was usually in the back room totaling sales and making payments to the local farmers where we purchase our produce. I love living in China. I love hearing my language, seeing the bright colors of tents and wares, and watching the little children playing games to occupy their time while their parents were shopping. What I wouldn't give to eat my mother's sweet and sour pork. My stomach growls just at the thought of it. I want so badly to go home but I can't, so I turn on the shower and try to wash away my misery. I step out of the bathroom with my hair wrapped up in a towel, and I'm trying desperately to hold back the tears that have started flowing. I take a deep breath and walk into our living room trying to pretend that everything is okay.

The room is empty, and I am relieved to see that Allie has gone to bed because I really don't want her to see me like this. I make a cup of tea and walk into the living room. I take a sip and relish in the taste of authentic tea. I put my cup down on the table and lean back on the couch and close my eyes. I am lost in my own thoughts and I jump when I hear the television click on. I look up and see Allie standing next to me with a quart of chocolate ice cream and an extra spoon. Sometimes I feel like Allie can read my mind. Allie's philosophy is that ice cream fixes everything. I smile, I can't help it, and I gratefully take the spoon as she plops down beside me. We don't need to talk. Instead we channel surf and settle for a comedy. It's so strange how our lives are so different, but we complement each other. We're exactly like yin and yang.

Chapter 4
Allie

The only good thing about being in college is the fact that I am now free to be myself. My parents have always thought (but never said) that I was odd. They would outwardly cringe when I didn't meet the status quo of the elite. What they could never understand is that I've never been comfortable with that type of lifestyle. I hated living in our huge mansion on the hill overlooking the city. I've always felt like Rapunzel being held hostage and never allowed to be free. I hated all of the elegant parties out by the pool that my parents constantly held. My mother always went over the top by hiring caterers, servers, and landscapers before every party. She even went so far as to have floating candles in the pool and lights strung around the gondola. Who does that? My parents call these parties networking, but I call it a complete waste of time. I never had the choice to not attend and I was expected to play the obedient child and paste on a smile, be polite, and make sure that I made a good impression.

Unfortunately for them I did have my moments of rebelling. There was one time when I had cut my own hair and I thought it looked great. I was so proud of myself that I ran to my mom's room and showed her, grinning from ear to ear. My mom on the other hand was outraged and I thought she might have a heart attack. She grabbed me by my arm and dragged me kicking and screaming to her salon to "fix" it. From that day on I was forced to grow my hair long. It was an unruly mess and took so much time to style. Ironically, my mom wears her hair short and cropped around her face. I smiled thinking that my parents would flip if they could see me now.

My parents made sure that I was enrolled in the best private schools and I hated every minute of it. The girls were full of drama. I mean like reality television drama. I stayed to myself most of the time. Of course, then the girls thought I was weird because I didn't associate with them, but I didn't care. Now that the nightmare of my childhood is over I am making a new start and can finally be me.

The first weekend I was away from home I stopped by the first salon I could find, and I had my dainty curls cut off up to my shoulders. Next, I dyed my boring brown hair with purple and blond highlights. I think it looks amazing and I feel more like myself. My parents keep sending me spending money each month, even though they were appalled when I chose to go to a public university. The money is supposed to be used for extra supplies. I'm not sure they would consider a new wardrobe "supplies" but that's what I need. I was suffocating trying to be a person that I'm not. If I had to describe my style it would be eclectic. I like bright and colorful clothes. I like long flowing skirts and tying scarves around my hair. Since I've been away from home I have multiple ear piercings plus a belly button ring, and lately I've been entertaining the idea of getting a butterfly tattoo on my shoulder. I sometimes get an eye roll or hear someone whisper as I walk past them. I know they're judging me but I brush it off. One thing that I've never understood is how people could judge me without ever speaking to me.

I've come to the conclusion that people put others into categories just by looking at them. For example, if you dress weird you must have issues and if you dress conservative people are friendlier. If people would just take the time to talk to you, which very rarely happens by the way, then they just may move you to another category. For example, if I were the judging type, which I'm not, just by looking around my Art class, I can surmise that there are the serious academics with their planners out and already perusing the syllabus which they printed off ahead of time. Then you have the party crowd who are taking this as an elective because its art, so it must be easy, right? You have the introverts, the extroverts, the perfectionists, and those who could care less. Somehow, I will be forced to interact with all of these people which is fine with me because I'm on my own journey and they have been placed in my path for a reason.

The professor is late, so I take out my sketch pad and begin to draw. Drawing is the window to my soul. I haven't really settled on my niche yet, once again it goes back to having to put everything in a category. I like abstract but I also like realism. I love vibrant colors but black and white has value as well. I'd like to think everything is connected and not separated into different little boxes.

So far, I like living on my own. It's freeing. I'm not completely living alone because I do have a roommate named Kym. She's from China and seems quiet but very nice. She's a business major. I'm not quite sure how a business major and an art major ended up together but, so far, we've gotten along fine. I smile when I think about the day Kym moved into the dorm with me. I was unpacking the only box that I had brought with me and pulled out my art portfolio. Each picture or sketch was like stepping back in time. Kym had glanced over and asked cautiously, "What is that?"

I had looked at her in surprise since this was more than she had ever said to me thus far. "This? It's my portfolio. Would you like to see it?"

"Sure," Kym replied.

We both sat side by side on the bed and I flipped the portfolio back to the beginning. Kym studied a photograph of a little girl around two years old. The background of the picture was black and white while the little girl was in color. She had curly brown locks underneath a bright yellow rain hat. Her face was looking towards the sky and she had the biggest smile on her face. It was raining, and the little girl was dressed in a bright yellow raincoat and red rubber boots stomping in a puddle. The picture captured the little girl's delight.

"This is amazing, Allie. I didn't know you were a photographer."

I looked at the picture and shrugged, "I'm not. I just see beauty around me and I want to capture it."

Kym carefully turned the page to a pastel drawing of a dahlia in full bloom. The vibrant purple and white colors jumped off the page. "Wow, Allie, you have a real talent. Your family must be really proud of you."

I remember nearly choking on a sip of coffee, "Not exactly. My parents wanted me to major in business because my father says business is what makes the world go around. He thinks my choice to be an interior designer is a complete waste of time."

Kym had looked at her clearly confused and asked, "Why are you becoming an interior designer instead of an artist? These are amazing!"

I had stood up and spread my arms encompassing our dorm room. "I love showing off beauty in the world and in people. I love taking a blank canvas and making it come to life. Can you imagine what I could do with a whole house?"

Kym giggled. "Well, when you put it that way I can see your point." She flipped through more pages and then asked, "How did you convince your family to let you pursue interior design?"

I still groan when I think about my family. "My parents only care about how people perceive them. They don't really care about reality, so I enrolled in Interior Design and told them I was majoring in Business with a minor in Interior Design. By the time I'm finished with my major which is only Interior Design and they discover I'm only an interior designer I'll already have applications in all over the country and none of them will include where they live."

I remember the sympathetic look Kym gave me when she said, "So I guess you're not very close with your family, huh?"

I can still feel the anger that boiled in the pit of my stomach. "Not in the least." I replied as I closed my portfolio and looked at Kym. "I didn't mean anything negative about being a business major. It's just not for me that's all."

Kym had rolled her eyes and smiled. "No offense taken. My father believes business makes the world go around too."

"Do you?" I had asked truly curious about my new roommate.

Kym smiled and shrugged. "In a way, yes. I'm good with numbers and it comes naturally to me. My father has had me working with numbers for most of my life. I even kept the books for my parents' business and I loved every minute of it. I like the challenge of keeping everything in balance."

That's when I knew we were destined to be great friends. Kym was genuine and real which was a refreshing change from the girls back home. It's funny but somehow Kym accepts all of my quirks and I accept her academic drive. Although we are exact opposites, I think we could learn a lot from each other.

I've met a few other people on campus. Some talk to me and others blatantly ignore me, which is fine by me. I'm a positive person and like to be surrounded by people who are positive as well. Jenna and Cara seem to be people I would like to know more. I think Jenna is a little like me, a free spirit, whereas Cara is a little more like Kym, the studious type. I'm not sure why I think that, it's just a feeling I get. I hope we can hang out more together. I like to know what other people's stories are. Where they grew up, what their families are like, what their interests are, things like that. Jenna seemed quiet at lunch, but I have a feeling that there's more there than what meets the eye.

While I'm sketching my phone rings. I look at the screen and see that it's Jeff. I roll my eyes and answer it. "Hey," I whisper into the phone. "Why are you whispering?" he asked.

"I'm sitting in class waiting for the instructor," I reply.

"Oh," he said laughing. "I guess I just lost $50. I bet Matt that you'd change your mind about taking classes and move on to something else before they started."

I roll my eyes. Jeff was my neighbor, or should I say partner in crime back home. We always did everything together, especially getting into trouble much to our parents' dismay. We both hated the affluent lifestyle. Don't get me wrong, Jeff loved the expensive red corvette that he raced up and down the road and all the other vast amenities he's acquired, but he hated the artificialness of it all. Jeff and I would spend countless hours sitting under the huge oak tree at the park down the road. We would look up at the stars and talk about the day we would get out of this absurd lifestyle of pretending to be people we're not. We even had a plan that after we graduated we were both going to drive out of the Stepford neighborhood and never look back.

I've always known that Jeff had a crush on me. When we got older he used to ask me out all the time, but I've always said no. Don't get me wrong, Jeff is HOT. His crystal blue eyes look right through you. His blond hair looks like he spends all of his time on the beach (which he does) and his tanned muscular body beckons you to want to touch. My friends say I'm an idiot for not dating Jeff, but the problem is that as perfect as Jeff is, inside and out, I'm not the settling down type and in the end, I would only hurt him. Not deliberately, of course. The fact is I've never had a relationship. Of course, I've had dates here and there but nothing more than that. I have my parents to thank for that.

They are not role model relationship material. To the public and their "network friends" they are the epitome of true love. They fawn over one another and appear to be madly in love. Some would even say the perfect couple. But once everyone left and the last candle was put out the fighting and bickering would begin. My dad would begin yelling and accusing my mom of flirting with every guy at the party, and my mom would accuse my dad of always being drunk, which then led to a glass or bottle being thrown against the wall and shattering into tiny bits and pieces. Next came the inevitable door slamming followed by a desolate silence. My parents have slept in separate rooms for the last five years.

To this day, I am amazed that the police have never been called to our house. When I was younger I used to hide in my closet with the door shut to drown out their voices. I would cry myself to sleep and hope that the demons would be gone in the morning. So, since my parents have been the only continuous relationship I have witnessed growing up, I decided at a very young age that I would never end up like that, and as I said before I would never put Jeff through anything like that. He deserves so much more and I'm not sure I could totally commit knowing how my parents' life has been.

"Okay, I'll make this quick," said Jeff. "How about we meet later tonight and catch up. I haven't seen you in a while and I miss you."

I look up and see that the instructor just walked into the classroom. "I'd like that," I replied. "When and where?"

"Mickey's Hideout at seven?" Jeff asked. "That would be halfway for both of us."

"I'll be there," I reply. "Gotta go." I hang up quickly, slipping my phone back into my bag and look down at the syllabus that has just landed on my desk.

Chapter 5
Mickey's Hideout

Allie walked into Mickey's Hideout right at seven p.m. She loved everything about this place especially the worn wooden floor- scuffed up by years of people dancing. This place wasn't like the hip hop nightclubs that scatter across the college towns. Instead, the interior was made of aged wood, and the main source of music came from a jukebox hanging on the wall unless it was a weekend when there's a live band. It has always been the favorite local honky-tonk for as long as Allie could remember. It was a place where everyone knew everyone. Allie smiled remembering a night all those years ago when Jeff had carved their initials into a tall wooden beam that ran along the wall next to the bar. He had taken out his knife and engraved *Jeff+Allie = Forever.* Allie looked over at the band warming-up on the stage and smiled. She and Jeff used to sneak in here with fake ID's long before she ever turned twenty-one.

It wasn't long before she spotted Jeff standing by a group of friends talking animatedly. He always drew a crowd no matter where he was. She waved at a few friends and walked up to the bar. Jackie was bartending tonight and stood at the other end of the bar wiping it down while talking to a young couple. Allie yelled over to her, "Jackie, can I have a beer?"

Jackie turned around and smiled at the sound of her voice. "Allie! Where have you been? I haven't seen you around for a while."

Allie shrugged, "Oh you know, busy."

Jackie looked over at Jeff and said, "Well, at least Jeff will be happy. He's been out of sorts since you've been gone."

Jackie leaned closer to Allie. "Just don't tell him I told you so."

Allie smiled and said, "No worries. I won't say a word."

Jackie handed her a beer as Allie pulled a wad of bills from her pocket. Jackie shook her head, "This one is on the house. Now get over there and quit making him wait." With beer in hand, Allie sauntered over to Jeff who had just turned around to greet her. "Hi, beautiful," he said, with a smile, as he wrapped his arms around her for a hug.

She hugged him back and kissed him on the cheek. "Hi yourself handsome." They walked over to a booth and plopped down. Allie slid off her coat and leaned back in her seat smiling. God how she had missed him. "So how was class?" Jeff asked.

Allie laughed. "Now you sound like my parents. Class was good. My roommate is good. Life is good. How about you?"

Jeff leaned back in his chair studying her and instead of answering her question said, “Something is different about you. I can’t quite pin down what it is though.”

Allie knew he was messing with her that was part of his charm. “Could it be my hair?” she asked bringing her hand up and combing her fingers through her tricolored ringlets.

“No, I don’t think so,” Jeff answered pretending to be perplexed by placing a finger over his lips.

Allie looked down at herself. “It must be my unique taste in clothing.”

Jeff slowly moved his gaze from the tip of her head down to her feet. Allie felt herself shiver under his appreciative assessment. He shook his head slowly, “Nope, I don’t think that’s it either.”

Allie laughed. “Okay, I give up.”

Jeff leaned closer, moving her hair to the side, inhaled then kissed her gently on the neck. “You’ve changed your perfume.”

Allie’s heart skipped a beat, and her breath hitched. She cleared her throat and said, “Oh that. I forgot about that.”

Damn he smells good. Jeff tilted his head so that his lips were hovering above hers. All she had to do was lean into him and she knew she’d be wrapped up in his arms and they would be devouring each other right here. Allie cleared her throat nervously and Jeff leaned slowly back against his seat. His eyes were penetrating. “So tell me, how are you really?”

Allie smiled. “Good, really, really good. I no longer have to pretend to be someone I’m not. I can dress like I want and act like I want. I love the freedom. It's just like we talked about Jeff. It's so good being away."

Jeff looked at her sadly and said, "You look happy. Freedom agrees with you."

She sipped from her beer and for a minute felt unexpectedly guilty. "I am. Being away from insanity agrees with me. How about you?"

She knew Jeff would always stay here in Kensington, which was part of the reason she never pursued a relationship with him. She needed more than this and he didn't.

He drew in a deep breath. "I'm good," Jeff replied. "I miss you, but work keeps me busy." Jeff's parents were not happy when Jeff decided to take the road less traveled and refused to go to college. Now he works at a local garage fixing vehicles and doing body work. Jeff loves every minute of it. He loves being able to take something that is broken and make it whole again. He is a natural when it comes to engines and he has a great reputation. The owner of the garage recognized this and had taken Jeff under his wing. He has slowly been teaching Jeff everything he knows so that one day Jeff could take over the garage.

Jeff intertwined his fingers with Allie's and looked at her smiling ruefully. "So you said you liked your roommate. What's she like?"

"Are you looking to get rid of me?" she asked teasingly.

Jeff looked at her with his deep blue eyes and said, "I could never get rid of you, Allie."

Her heart skipped a beat and she took another sip of beer then changed the subject. "My roommate's name is Kym and she's from China. She's a business major, kind of quiet, always studying, and she is an excellent cook."

"Well, that is the opposite of you. I'm surprised you two get along so well," Jeff replied, laughing.

"I know, right?" Allie laughed. "Maybe I can convince her to take a study break and I'll bring her along next time."

"That sounds like fun but to be honest she doesn't sound like my type," Jeff replied motioning to the waitress to bring another round of beers.

"Probably not, but she doesn't know many people and she is very homesick. Now if you're looking for someone more your type that would be Jenna."

The waitress brought over two more beers. "I doubt that, Allie. You're the only girl for me. Always have, always will be."

She smiled and took another swig of beer. "Well, to be honest I really don't know her very well, but something tells me that you would like her."

The bar door banged opened, and three big burly guys came bounding through. They were a rowdy bunch as they made their way to the bar. "Hey, Jackie, baby, get us some beers and throw in some shots too!"

Jackie walked over and said, "Hal, looks like you've been celebrating. What's the occasion?"

Hal smiled and said, "My wife left me and I'm a free man."

The other two guys with him started cheering him on. Jackie set a beer in front of each man along with a shot. Hal stopped her. "Wait a minute Jackie. The beers are for all of us, but the shots are for me, honey." He eyed Jackie. "What time do you get off?"

Jackie laughed. "Hal, I'm a married woman you know that."

Hal leaned over the bar. "My wife was a married woman too, but she still fooled around on the side." The guys with him laughed as Jackie just shook her head and walked over to refill someone's drink.

Allie looked over towards the bar and shook her head before looking back at Jeff. "See what I mean, Jeff. Relationships are destined to fail."

Jeff laughed and said, "College has made you jaded Allie."

Allie shot back, "My parents made me jaded."

Jeff shook his head and changed the subject. This had been a long-standing disagreement they had all the time. Allie looked at Jeff and felt her heart melt. She loved spending time with him. He made her laugh and he felt like home. Allie glanced down at her watch and Jeff saw the expression on her face. "Don't tell me, princess, it's the witching hour and you have to leave before you turn into a pumpkin."

She laughed. "You are correct. I have an early class in the morning and I'm not a morning person as it is."

"At least let's have one last dance," Jeff said holding his hand out waiting to lead her to the dance floor.

Allie smiled. “Okay, just one then I have to go.”

They walked through the crowd and stepped onto the dance floor. He wrapped his arms around her and pulled her close. She didn’t mind. She loved feeling his arms wrapped around her. They danced, silently lost in each other until Hal walked over and tapped Jeff on his shoulder. “May I dance with your lady?”

Jeff looked surprised and looked at Allie. Jeff was about to say no but Allie shrugged and broke away from Jeff. Hal took her in his arms and pulled her too close for comfort. Allie knew Jeff wasn’t happy, but she also knew that you can’t reason with a drunk. She didn’t see the harm in one little dance if that would pacify him.

Jeff went over and sat at the bar talking to Jackie who handed him two shots which he downed instantly. His eyes never left Allie and his temper was starting to boil. The song was coming to an end and Allie tried to pull away. Hal had other ideas and grabbed her head and kissed her. She tried to push him away from her, but he was too strong. The combination of sweat and alcohol permeated Allie’s senses. Jeff jumped off his chair and was by Allie’s side in an instant. He grabbed Hal and punched him first in the gut and then in the face. Hal fell back and laid on the floor in a daze. Hal’s two friends saw the commotion and jumped into action ready to help their friend. They both stood looking at Jeff braced for a fight.

Jeff could feel his anger boiling seeing Allie in another man’s arms and after she was taken advantage of he was seething. He faced them both with fire blazing in his eyes and fists clenched. The first man, a big burly giant, was twice Jeff's size, but he didn't care. He waited until the man came towards him, his whole body tense. He reared his fist back ready to strike but was caught off guard when the other brawny guy jumped in and held him still as the burly giant pummeled him.

"Stop!" Allie screamed. She was trying to pull the burly giant away from Jeff.

Jackie walked over with a wooden baseball bat held menacingly over her head and the rest of the bar patrons backing her up. "Break it up!" Jackie yelled threateningly.

Both men stopped and looked at Jackie. "You saw who started it Jackie. I'm just helping out a friend." He raised his fist ready to strike Jeff again.

Jackie stood her full five feet two and said, "Not in my bar you aren't. Now get going. All of you!"

The three men glared at Jeff but turned to leave. Jeff stood with blood dripping over his eye. Jackie looked at Jeff and grumbled, "Come on, let's get you cleaned up."

Jeff and Allie followed Jackie to the back kitchen. Jackie took out a plastic bag and filled it with ice then wrapped a bar rag around it. "Go on and clean that cut up and then put some ice on it," Jackie ordered. Jeff knew better than to argue and did as she said.

Allie picked up the bag of ice and put it on Jeff's eye which was already beginning to turn colors. "Ow, easy there Allie," Jeff winced.

Allie was fuming. "I will not take it easy. Jesus, Jeff what the hell were you thinking? You are such an idiot!"

Jeff pulled away and looked at her. He could not believe what he was hearing. "I'm an idiot? I wasn't the one who said yes to a dance with someone who was clearly intoxicated!"

Allie glared at him. "I was trying to de-escalate the situation so that it wouldn't turn into a bar fight."

"Well, that plan backfired," Jeff said sarcastically.

Allie was exasperated. "Well, it wouldn't have backfired if you would have just let things be. I'm not a damsel in distress you know. I can take care of myself."

Jeff looked at her dumbfounded. "It sure didn't look like you were taking care of yourself a minute ago. It looked like he was taking care of you or maybe I was mistaken and that's what you wanted."

Allie slapped him across the face and threw down the bag of ice she had been holding on his eye. They stared at each other until Jeff said, "Allie..." She turned and walked out of the room. Jeff jumped up and began to run after her. "Allie, wait! I'm sorry let's talk this out!"

Jackie shook her head as she watched Jeff follow Allie out the door. Allie clicked the fob to unlock her door and quickly got in and started up the car. Jeff was standing next to the car trying to open the door to keep her from leaving. She instantly locked the door and put her car in reverse.

"Allie, stop! You're being ridiculous. Let's just talk okay?"

Allie refused to look at him and instead stomped on the gas which caused the car to shoot out of its parking space sending gravel flying. He shielded himself with his arms and ran to stand in front of her car to prevent her from leaving but she stomped on the gas forcing him to jump out of the way or be hit. She pulled out of the parking lot leaving Jeff standing alone watching her taillights fade out of sight. He picked up a rock and threw it towards her car in frustration, but she was too far gone. "Damn it!" he yelled throwing his hands up in the air. He took a deep breath and stomped back into the bar.

Jackie looked at him with sympathy. "A double shot of tequila, Jackie," he grumbled.

Jackie looked at Jeff and said, "I think you've had enough Jeff. Why don't you just go on home."

He looked at her incredulously but didn't argue. Instead he picked up his jacket, turned, and walked out the door.

Chapter 6
Jenna

BEEP, BEEP, BEEP. Jenna rolled over and turned off the annoying blaring of the alarm for the third time. She looked at the time and groaned. She hastily got up, threw on some clothes that she hoped were clean, and hurried out the door. Although she was minutes away from being late to class she stopped by the cafeteria for a quick coffee to take with her. She stepped through the door of her classroom just as the instructor was about to begin.

"That's cutting it close," Cara whispered.

Jenna looked at her and held up a cup of coffee with a triumphant smile.

"You look like you just rolled out of bed," Cara whispered looking up at Jenna.

"I did."

Cara giggled, "You really aren't a morning person are you."

The instructor sent us a warning look and we both stopped talking. Jenna was surprised to admit that she really liked her Psychology class. It was interesting learning about the mind and how it affects people's behavior. Jenna and Cara diligently took notes about an upcoming project, inwardly groaning at the amount of time and effort this project will require.

At the end of class Jenna looked down at her disheveled appearance. She had an hour before her next class which gave her just enough time to go home and look presentable before it started. The two girls walked out of class together. Cara lit her cigarette just as we left the building.

"You're killing me with that stuff," Jenna remarked, coughing in exaggeration.

"I'm the one inhaling so don't give me your lecture about me killing you with my smoking," Cara retorted.

"I'm inhaling your second-hand smoke," Jenna replied, frantically fanning her hand in front of her face.

Cara rolled her eyes. "Well, I'm inhaling the scent of you without a shower," she said, fanning her hand in front of her face.

"If this class didn't start so early then maybe I'd have time for a shower," Jenna replied, smelling herself to see if Cara was joking.

Cara looked at her watch and put out her cigarette. "Well, I'm off to my next class." She picked up her backpack and slung it over her shoulder.

Jenna picked up her bag and asked, "You want to meet up later for dinner?"

As if on cue, Cara's stomach started to rumble, and she pulled out a granola bar that she saw sticking out of Jenna's bag. She peeled back the wrapper and took a bite, “Sure. See you then.” With food in hand she turned around and began heading to her next class.

Cara waved to me as she walked into the cafeteria and dropped her stuff at our usual table. “I ***need*** a latte,” she grumbled and made a beeline to the nearest vendor. She didn’t look any happier with latte in hand when she plopped down at the table.

“What’s wrong?” Jenna asked sympathetically.

“What isn’t wrong,” Cara replied grumpily. “Every class I’ve been to today has some project due. I swear I think all the professors get together to see how to make our lives as miserable as possible. Plus, this week I have a huge presentation to present with my group and even though I have loved every minute I’m so exhausted when I get home that I don’t have the energy for homework. And on top of that, every time I call Trent he keeps blowing me off.”

“Wow,” Jenna remarked. “Rough day.”

“Yep,” Cara said taking a sip of her latte. “I hate living on a dry campus because I could definitely use a drink today.”

“I thought I’d see you two here,” Allie said as she pulled out a chair and sat down. She held a heaping plate of cheese fries. Jenna’s mouth watered as Allie placed the plate in the middle of the table. She looked at Jenna, smiled, and said, “Help yourself.” Jenna didn’t need to be told twice. She grabbed one and popped it into her mouth. It tasted heavenly.

Cara looked at the fries and was about to go on a rampage about eating fried foods when Jenna quickly interceded. "Hi Allie, I was wondering when you were going to show up."

"I would have been here sooner, but I was trying to talk Kym into taking a break and coming out with me. As you can tell I didn't succeed. She refused to leave the dorm saying she had too much homework to do. I tried to tell her that all work and no play make for a dull girl."

Cara mumbled, "I know exactly how she feels."

Allie started to grab another fry when her cell phone rang. She pulled the phone out of her pocket and looked at the caller ID. She frowned and clicked it off sending it to voice mail.

"You don't look happy. Who was that?" Cara asked concerned for her friend.

Allie grumbled, "Just a salesman. No big deal." Fifteen minutes later her phone rang again and once again she sent it to voice mail.

Jenna looked at her friend. "That's a pretty persistent salesman you have there. Maybe you should answer it and tell him you're not interested."

Allie grumbled, "Oh he's persistent all right. And believe me I'm NOT interested in anything he has to say." Allie grabbed another fry and stood up to leave. "I'll see you girls later. I'm going for a walk."

"Wow," said Cara. "Allie looks miserable. I wonder what's going on?"

"I don't know," Jenna said. "But I've figured a way to find out."

Cara looked at her dubiously. "Maybe we shouldn't get involved. I'm sure she'll work it out."

Jenna held up Allie's cell phone. "How did you get that?" Cara asked astonished.

Jenna laughed. "You really don't want to know." She looked at the screen and found the number that kept calling Allie. Jenna pushed redial and waited for an answer.

Cara whispered, "Jenna don't. It's none of our business!"

Jenna held up a finger as someone on the other end picked up. "Thank God, Allie! I've been worried sick about you!" the voice on the other end exclaimed.

Jenna spoke, "This isn't Allie and why would you be worried sick about her. What's going on? Why are you harassing her?"

Jeff was silent at first then spoke, "Who is this and why do you have Allie's phone?"

Jenna looked at Cara and then spoke into the phone, "You answer my questions first then I'll answer yours." Cara looked like she was about to faint.

"Fine," Jeff replied. "My name is Jeff, and Allie is a good friend of mine. Now it's your turn to answer my question. Who are you?"

"Jenna," she replied.

Jeff's tone changed. "Oh, Jenna! I'm Jeff."

Jenna rolled her eyes. "You've already said that."

"Sorry," Jeff replied. "Allie mentioned you to me last weekend when we were together. Apparently, she has failed to mention *me* to any of *her* friends."

Jenna wasn't giving him any leeway. "If you're such a great friend why do you keep harassing her? I'm sometimes a little slow to get a hint but if I kept getting sent to voice mail then I would eventually get the idea that Allie doesn't want to talk to me. So, what did you do to my friend?"

Jeff was silent for a minute, and then breathed out a long sigh. "I made a mistake and now she's mad at me and refuses to listen to anything I say. I keep calling her to apologize."

"Apologize for what?" Jenna asked skeptically. She wasn't going to make this easy on him.

"Apologize for being a jealous idiot and getting into a bar fight which I didn't start just for the record. Now can I talk to Allie? I just want to apologize that's all."

Jenna could hear the remorse in his voice and began to feel sorry for him. "Sorry Jeff, she's not here."

Now Jeff was skeptical. "Then why do you have Allie's phone?"

Jenna cringed and said, "It's a long story."

"I have time," Jeff replied.

"I don't," Jenna replied. "But I do have an idea."

"Like give Allie her phone back that you lifted off of her?" Jeff accused.

"I wasn't stealing it. I just wanted to know why you keep harassing her. She's my friend and she's miserable."

Jeff said, "Look Jenna. We both obviously care about Allie and want her to be happy. I just want to apologize that's all. I swear."

Jenna looked at Cara who was about to combust with curiosity. Jenna spoke again, "How about if you apologize in person? The only catch is that I'm going to be there too, and if you so much as make a move on my friend or cause her any more unhappiness then you're going to have to deal with me, and trust me you don't want to go there."

Jeff laughed. "Deal. I just want to talk to her and apologize that's all. How about Saturday night at seven?"

"Okay," Jenna replied. "You picked the night and the time, so I'll pick the place. Mulcahey's Pub, it's by the college."

Jeff sounded confused. "I don't attend the college and I'm not from around there. Can you give me directions?"

Jenna shook her head and laughed. "If you want to see Allie then I suggest you Google it." She clicked off Allie's phone and dropped it in her purse. "That should keep him from calling her for the rest of the week."

Cara looked at Jenna astounded. "I can't believe you just did that!"

Jenna looked at her and said, "*We*. We did that. Cara, we have to make sure that Allie is at Mulcahey's at seven. He says he's a friend of Allie's and just wants to apologize. We're going to make sure that is all he does. I can't stand seeing Allie so sad all the time."

Cara agreed, "Neither can I."

Saturday night came quickly, and all the girls gathered back at their usual table. Cara slammed her phone down on the table.

"Rough day?" Allie asked.

"Rough week," replied Cara.

"So, what are you girls planning to do this weekend?" Allie asked.

Cara frowned and said, "Nothing any more. I was supposed to go to Trent's this weekend, but he says he's got rotations and that I shouldn't come because we wouldn't spend any time together."

Jenna looked at her sympathetically and laughed inwardly. Cara would have made a great actress.

"Allie, do you have plans?" Jenna asked, going back to the topic at hand.

Allie shook her head. "The only plan I have is to sleep for two whole days. I really need a break from everything."

Jenna smiled and said, "Well, before you do that why don't we go out to Mulcahey's for a while. I want to go out and forget about this miserable week, but I don't want to go out by myself."

Cara smiled. "I'm game. I haven't had a drink since forever and I could really use one."

Allie finished her latte and said, "Count me in. Like I said, I need a break."

They all looked at Kym who was quietly eating her dinner. "What?" she asked.

"Nothing," replied Allie. "But you need to stop eating and get dressed we're leaving in an hour."

Everyone agreed to meet at Jenna's dorm at six thirty and then walk the two blocks to the pub. They were all in good spirits as they walked through the pub door. Kym saw two business students and walked over to say hi. Allie and Cara grabbed a table while Jenna went to grab them each a beer. The music was blasting from the jukebox and the girls immediately started to relax. It wasn't long before they found themselves out on the dance floor. A slow song came on and Allie immediately recognized it as one of her and Jeff's favorite songs. She started to walk off the dance floor until she felt a tap on her shoulder and she turned around.

Her eyes grew wide when she saw Jeff standing there, holding out his hand. He gave her a lopsided smile and she took his hand. He held her in his arms and whispered in her ear, "I'm so sorry Allie. I would never hurt you and I was an ass. Could you ever find it in your heart to forgive me?"

Allie was quiet for a minute and nodded her head as they swayed to the music. "I never could stay mad at you, just don't be such a jerk tonight okay?"

Jeff smiled. "You have my word."

They continued to dance, and Allie asked, "How did you know I was going to be here tonight anyway? This is a long way from home for you."

He smiled. "Just a lucky guess. I'm glad I wasn't wrong."

Jenna and Cara stood watching the dancing couple and gave each other a high five. The song ended, and Allie and Jeff walked hand in hand back to the table where Jenna and Cara were sipping their beer.

"Jeff, I'd like you to meet my friends." She pointed to Cara first, "This is Cara, and this is Jenna."

Jeff lifted an eyebrow at Jenna and smiled. "Hello ladies. I'm really glad to meet you. Any friend of Allie's is a friend of mine."

Jenna watched the way he looked at Allie and knew he was head over heels in love with her. Poor guy!

Chapter 7

Moving Out

Jenna looked at her reflection in the mirror. She was glad to be getting off campus and going out with the girls. They hadn't been able to get together for the past three weeks and it felt like a lifetime. Jenna inspected her tight-fitting jeans and smoothed down her light blue shirt that left little to the imagination. She leaned forward and applied her lipstick, gave her hair one more quick brush through, and turned to leave.

Allie, Kym, and Cara were all talking and waiting at the car when she walked up. "Wow," said Allie. "Jeff and the guys are going to love you!"

Jenna laughed. "I haven't been out in forever and I don't know when I will again. I thought the occasion warranted a little dressing up."

Jenna climbed into the back of the car and listened to Allie tell stories of her rebellious escapades with Jeff while her parents were "networking." Jenna closed her eyes and thought about her rebellious escapades. She didn't intentionally set out to be rebellious. She was only having fun, but it didn't seem that way to her parents. She couldn't help but smile when she thought about all the late-night parties she used to sneak out to.

She remembered the yellow glowing lights illuminating from every window when she pulled into the driveway. She recalled clouds of cigarette smoke along with the pungent smell of weed lingering through the air. Once the party was hopping there would invariably be someone puking in the bushes. All party houses were the same. Each house contained underage teenagers laughing and shouting to one another in order to be heard above the music. It didn't matter which house Jenna was at because the minute she walked through the door she always felt at home. The wooden kitchen table would be lined up with stacks of red plastic cups, all ready to be filled with a vast array of alcohol that kids would sneak out of their parents' cabinets. Girls dressed in tight fitting clothes would be eyeing up the guys while sipping on beer but not Jenna. Beer was for wusses, if you are going to drink then go big or go home, that has always been her motto. She could throw back shots with the best of them and then she would dance. As she danced she could feel the eyes of every guy in the room watching her every move. Her hips would sway to the rhythm of the music. It felt liberating and the combination gave her a special kind of high. The night Jacob had taken her in his arms and pulled her close to him while they swayed to the music showed her that she was no longer looked upon as too young.

Jacob was tall with broad shoulders. His smoldering blue eyes and dimples would melt any heart. His strong hands slowly slid from Jenna's back to her bottom. He pulled Jenna closer to him. Her heart had fluttered when he leaned down and brought his mouth to hers and began thoroughly kissing her. When the song ended he had gently taken her by the hand and led her upstairs. They found an empty bedroom and closed the door. Jenna giggled as Jacob stumbled and then fell into bed beside her. Jenna didn't remember much after that, but she would never forget waking up the next morning and discovering that she was no longer a virgin and to top it off she was left lying alone in a strange bedroom. Tears slid down her face when she realized what had happened. She jumped out of bed and quickly got dressed then walked down the stairs not wanting to draw attention to herself. "Hey, there's our party girl," one of Jacob's friends cheered. After that Jenna was always referred to as the party girl. Most of the other girls would roll their eyes and hated her. Jenna could care less, she shrugged it off and hung out with the guys. They didn't seem to mind and after a while she got used to going by the name Party Girl and wore it as a badge of honor. She was one of them and she made sure she partied with the best of them every chance she got.

Jenna snapped back to reality when they pulled into the gravel parking lot of Mickey's Hideaway. It was in the middle of nowhere which seemed like an odd place to have a bar. Looking around the parking lot at the vast number of cars that were parked there, the bar surprisingly seemed to draw a big crowd. Jenna opened the car door already anticipating a good time. She scanned the front of the building where a wooden porch held two round tables with people laughing, along with the smell of greasy fried food wafting through the air. There was an illuminated open sign flashing in the window, beckoning them to come inside.

The sound of a live band seeped outside, and Jenna was already itching to get onto the dance floor. Cara clicked the fob to lock her car and the girls walked towards the bar together. They opened the door and Allie made a beeline for a group of guys standing at the bar drinking beer. Allie and Jeff wrapped their arms around each other and Allie kissed him lightly on the cheek. His arm remained resting on the small of her back as she turned and said grinning, "Ladies, you remember Jeff."

Oh I remember Jeff alright thought Jenna. Jeff looked at her with those piercing blue eyes and her heart skipped a beat. She knew if she continued to look into them he would see right into her soul. Jenna smiled nonchalantly and looked away taking in the rest of the bar. Although Jenna thrived on having a good time, she would never do it at a friend's expense. Allie came first.

Jeff cleared his throat and then introduced his friends. Everyone ordered a round of beer then our group broke up into smaller groups. Kym looked uncomfortable but was talking to Jeff's friend, Jamal, who was listening intently to something she was saying. Jenna watched as he said something back to her and when she saw Kym burst out in laughter Jenna slowly began to relax.

Allie grabbed Jenna's arm and directed her to sit with her and Jeff. Jeff had positioned himself at the bar between Allie and Jenna. "Well, Allie, you're looking as beautiful as the last time I saw you." He hugged her again.

Jenna felt like a third wheel and was just about to leave but Allie grabbed her arm. "Stay here with us Jenna. Jeff is a huge flirt but he's harmless." She looked into his deep blue eyes and she could feel her breath hitch. She wasn't so sure that he was as harmless as Allie suggested.

Jenna began to feel more at ease after a couple of beers and she discovered that Jeff was extremely funny and had her laughing so hard that her stomach hurt. It wasn't long before they were all doing shots and Jenna could feel the music pulling her towards the dance floor. Jenna stood up and walked over to Cara who was sitting alone at a table texting on her phone to Trent. She looked miserable. "Cara, forget about him for tonight. It's a girls' night out. Let's have fun."

Cara sighed in frustration and set her phone down on the table "I know. It's just frustrating. Trent and I used to talk all the time and now I can hardly get a hold of him. I just really miss him you know?"

Jenna grabbed Cara's hand to drag her out onto the dance floor and said, "He's busy. Let's have a little fun. Who knows when we'll get away to do this again."

Cara sighed with resignation. "Fine. Trent's not answering any of my texts anyway." Cara slid her phone into her back pocket as Jenna led her to the dance floor. The girls' bodies swayed to the beat of the music and all of life's worries began to fade away. Allie and Kym joined them and soon they were all dancing to the music and laughing.

Jenna glanced back at Jeff who was bobbing his head and watching the girls dance. That smile of his could melt an entire glacier. His eyes zeroed in on Jenna and she began to feel self-conscious which was unexpected. She turned around so that she could no longer see him even though she could still feel his eyes boring a hole through her. Finally, the song ended, and Jenna looked over and saw that Jeff and his friends had gathered back at the bar. Jeff was talking and he soon had them bursting out in laughter. The music started up again and she tried to lose herself and forget about the flutter in her chest. She hasn't been this attracted to a person in a very long time, but Jenna quickly came back to reality when she heard Kym laugh and say, "Allie, I have never had this much fun. Thank you for making me come along."

Allie put her arm around her and said, "This is only the beginning my friend. We will make many fun memories together."

Once the song ended they sidled up to the bar just as the bartender announced that it was closing time. Everyone begged for just one last round of drinks, and Allie gave the bartender her sexiest smile. Jeff laughed and shook his head as the bartender served up one more round. Allie always seemed to get what she wanted.

The girls finished their drinks and slipped on their jackets. It was starting to get colder out. Jenna shivered a little as they walked out the door and Jeff plopped his arm over Jenna's shoulders. "I had fun tonight," he said.

She looked up at him and smiled. "So did I." She loved the feel of him so close to her.

Cara walked quickly over to the car and started warming it up. It had been a great night. Allie walked over towards Jenna and Jeff removed his arm and gave Allie a big hug. She hugged him back and gave him a quick kiss then he whispered in her ear, "One day Allie you won't want to walk away." Allie's heart skipped a beat and she pulled away and laughed to lighten the mood. Allie turned and lifted her arm in the air in a wave and walked to the car. Jenna's heart sank as she and Kym said their goodbyes and followed Allie.

On the long ride home, Kym was extremely talkative thanks to the alcohol, and began to open up to everyone about her family and the pressure she was under to establish herself in America. "I also have a boyfriend," Kym confided blushing.

"What?" We all shouted in unison. "Why haven't we heard about this before?"

Kym shifted uncomfortably in her seat. "No one else knows about us except Allie." She glanced over at her friend. "His name is Chao and he took over my job at the market. I think I'm in love with him, but my parents will never approve."

Jenna looked at her stunned. "Why not? He sounds like he's kind, hardworking, and if he managed to get your attention he's got to be amazing."

Kym wiped a tear from her cheek. "He is, but my parents want me to meet someone here in America. They do not want me to go back to China. Chao wrote to me and told me that he has joined the People's Liberation Army and is now a soldier. He did this to impress my parents and I can no longer talk to him because now he is in training."

Allie put her arm around Kym. "It'll work out, you'll see. Everyone is doing this because they love you. When the time is right everything will come together, and you will know what to do."

Kym leaned her head onto Allie's shoulder. "I hope you're right. I miss them all so much. I feel so far away from everyone I love."

Jenna tried to lighten the mood. "Well, at least you have us."

Everyone laughed, and it wasn't long before we were back to grumbling about dorm life, homework, and bad food.

"It's too bad that we can't all live together," Jenna groaned. "We seem to always be together anyway."

"Why don't we?" Allie asked.

Jenna laughed. "Yeah, like that's going to happen. It would have been fun though!"

"Why not?" Allie persisted. "Just because you have a dorm room doesn't mean you have to live in it. You said yourself that you never see your roommate. Let's get a place of our own. It doesn't have to be complicated."

Jenna smiled as the idea manifested and she said excitedly, "I love the idea of having roommates. Count me in."

Kym squealed with delight. "I love the idea of living like a family."

Cara was quiet, and Jenna knew she hadn't listened to any of their conversation. Lately, her world revolved around Trent. Jenna had never met him, but she had a feeling that she wouldn't like him very much. Each week Cara was more miserable than she was the week before. Jenna was really starting to worry about her.

The car grew quiet as they all started winding down and becoming tired. Jenna turned on the radio. The song, 'Lean on Me', was playing and she started singing along with the radio. Allie joined in and then eventually Kym. Jenna gently leaned towards Cara and started singing louder. Cara laughed and joined in. Once the song was over Allie said, "We should definitely do it."

"Do what?" Cara asked.

"All move in together," Allie said excitedly. "It would be so much fun! We could help each other with homework. We could take turns cooking. It would be so great!"

Cara was quiet as we continued to try and convince her. "We'd have our own place instead of meeting up in the cafeteria." Cara was still quiet.

"Cara?" Allie asked. "Are you in?"

Cara had a sad smile on her face and said, "Count me out ladies. I'm fine where I am."

Jenna looked incredulously at Cara, "You're kidding right? You are so NOT fine where you are. Your roommate is a slob and she constantly has parties. You hate to be there and on most nights you study in a noisy cafeteria. Come on, move in with us."

Cara was quiet for a moment and then said, "It wouldn't be fair to you guys. I'll be going to Trent's most weekends. I'll only be here during the week and with my rotations at the hospital starting next semester I'll be gone a lot."

Jenna almost spoke but kept her thoughts to herself. She was pretty sure Cara would not be going to Trent's most weekends.

Everyone went quiet as the radio started playing, 'We Are Family'. Jenna couldn't help it, it was like a sign. Jenna started singing and slowly everyone but Cara joined in.

The girls sang louder and louder until finally Cara threw up her hands and said, "Fine! I'll move in with you guys but I'm not promising you that I'll be there much. Are you happy now?"

They all screamed excitedly as Cara pulled into the dorm parking lot.

Chapter 8
Cara

Cara walked into the house carrying a bag of groceries and plopped them on the counter. "Okay, Kym I think I've got everything on your list."

Kym looked over her shoulder at Cara while sautéing broccoli, onions, and carrots in a wok on the stove. "I was wondering when you were going to show up. Hand me the soy sauce, will you?" Kym asked.

Cara reached into the bag and brought it over to her. "That smells amazing," Cara said plucking a piece of broccoli out of the pan and popping it into her mouth. "I love vegetarian night."

Kym is an amazing cook and Cara has told her over and over that she should switch her major from business to culinary. "You would be an unbelievable chef." Cara reminded Kym again.

Unlike Kym, Cara could not cook at all. In fact, the last time she tried to cook they ended up throwing the pan away because it was burnt on the bottom and the food was unrecognizable. That night everyone had pizza instead. Cara had already decided that her life would consist of living on takeout food in between shifts at the hospital. So far, her rotations have been interesting because every two weeks she moves to a different wing of the hospital. So far, she's worked in emergency and maternity. Now she is assigned to working in the oncology wing of the hospital. At first she had mixed emotions about working in oncology because it reminded her of her grandmother and everything she had gone through, but now she has discovered that she loves the hustle and bustle and most of all she loves the patients that she works with even the grumpy ones.

Her favorite patient is Sam who is seventy-five and suffers from esophageal cancer. He is waiting to have surgery, but you wouldn't know it from the twinkle in his eye. He is such a positive person and he can tell a story like no one else. She can't remember anyone who makes her laugh so hard. Sam is also a big flirt, but all the nurses love him, and to be honest everyone tends to spoil Sam a lot.

Madeline is another patient of hers. She is only twenty-three and she has the most beautiful little curly haired girl with big blue eyes who comes to visit her almost every day. Madeline suffers from Stage one breast cancer. She is lucky to have caught it so early. Madeline has decided to have her breast removed so that she does not have to worry about the cancer spreading. She says her daughter is much more important to her than her breasts. Cara agrees and it's great to see that Madeline has a wonderful support system around her. Cara's beginning to think that oncology may be her niche.

Kym looked at Cara and asked, "Are you working tonight?"

Cara walked over and plopped on the couch picking up the remote. "Nope. For once I can relax and unwind."

Kym smiled. "I'm glad. Lately, we haven't seen much of you."

Cara groaned and shook her head walking back to the stove to grab another piece of broccoli. "I know. I'm really glad you guys convinced me to move in with you but don't say I didn't warn you about not being around much."

Kym smiled. "I know but for the record I'm really glad you're here."

Cara smiled. "Me too, the only thing that would make this day better is if Trent would call me back."

"When was the last time you've seen him?" Kym asked.

"Seen who?" Jenna asks as she walks in and sits beside Cara.

"Trent," Cara replied exasperated. "I haven't seen him in three weeks. I called him to ask when I can drive out to see him and he always says he's really busy and his workload is intense. Lately, he's been helping out in the emergency room and when I do talk to him it seems like his mind is elsewhere. I'm trying not to let it bother me but it's really beginning to."

"Come on," Jenna said encouragingly. "Let's go for a walk and you can tell me all about it."

Cara blinked away the tears that were starting to well in her eyes and let out a shaky breath. She really didn't want to talk about it at all but Jenna always has a way of making things seem better, so she slipped on her coat and they walked outside. Cara pulled a cigarette out of the pack and Jenna held up the lighter with the flame already lit. Cara laughed and leant in to light up. They walked slowly down to the lake which wasn't far from their house.

"Guys are jerks. You're better off without them," Cara grumbles.

Jenna looked over at her and smiles. "Not all the time."

Cara studied her and saw that something was different. "What is that supposed to mean?"

"It means that you and Trent have been together for a very long time. Didn't you say you were high school sweethearts?"

Cara took another drag off her cigarette. "Yeah."

"Well, if you two survived the hellish nightmare of high school then this will be a piece of cake," Jenna explained confidently. Even though at the moment Jenna really didn't like Trent and had a feeling he was cheating she continued, "It's just that right now you are both stressed. I'm assuming you are both intense people and it's hard to focus on a million different things right now. You need to give each other a break. It's okay to be busy. It's okay to be distracted sometimes. It doesn't mean he doesn't love you."

Cara blew out a long breath. "You're right, I'm just being stupid. It just seems like the longer we're apart the less we have to say to each other. I'm worried that's all."

They sat quietly on the bench both lost in their own thoughts watching two toddlers throwing bread into the water and squealing in delight when two ducks swim over to eat it. Cara looked at Jenna and nudged her. "What's happened to you?"

"What do you mean?" she asked.

"I mean, you have been so positive lately. You're always smiling like the cat who ate the canary. Something is up. Spill it."

"Well, it might have something to do with a certain guy I've been texting with."

"Is it someone I know?" Cara asked excitedly.

"Actually, yes but you can't say anything."

Cara nodded her head in agreement the curiosity killing her.

"It's Jeff," Jenna said nervously.

"What? Jeff, as in Allie's Jeff?" Cara exclaimed in surprise.

Jenna rolled her eyes. "It's not like that, not really anyway. We're just friends and according to Jeff that's all that he and Allie are. He admitted that he's always had feelings for Allie, but that Allie has always made it clear that she would never be in a relationship with him. We're just talking that's all."

Cara looked at Jenna closely. "Are you sure that's all? Allie's our friend."

Jenna stood up and let out a breath of exasperation. "Yes, that's all. I'm not like that. I would never hurt Allie. I can't believe you would think that low of me."

Cara stood up and faced Jenna. “I know you wouldn’t hurt Allie. Just be careful. I don’t want to see you or Allie hurt.”

Jenna was fuming why couldn’t Cara just be happy for her? Jenna shot back, “Don’t worry about me I’m a big girl and I know how to take care of myself. Maybe you should take a lesson.”

“What is that supposed to mean?” Cara asked indignantly.

Jenna walked over to her with her hands on her hips. “Oh, come on, Cara, open your eyes. Trent’s not that busy. He’s cheating on you!”

Their voices rose higher and the mother of the two little girls feeding the ducks walked over to her daughters and guided the girls towards the playground and away from the commotion.

Cara looked at Jenna incredulously. “You don’t know him! You are just jealous because you don’t have a relationship like Trent and I have. He would never do that.”

Jenna laughed. “You can’t be serious! Girl, he’s playing you and you’re letting him get away with it.”

Cara started to walk away but Jenna called after her, “Cara open your eyes! Nobody’s that busy. He’s always at the hospital? He’s always studying? I’m the girl that boyfriend’s go to when they cheat on their girlfriend! He’s cheating on you.”

Cara was speechless then turned and walked up to Jenna and said in a low threatening tone, “Stay the hell away from me!”

Jenna took a step back and laughed. "Cara, you don't have to worry about me. You have nothing worth having." Jenna turned around and started walking back home leaving Cara standing alone.

Jenna walked into the house and slammed the door. Kym was about to ask if she wanted dinner but after seeing the expression on Jenna's face she decided not to. She turned the stir fry down to simmer and waited for the rest of the girls to get home. Allie came home next, "Oh my gosh, Kym, that smells amazing!" She looked around. "Where are the other girls?"

Kym smiled wryly and said, "Well, Jenna just stomped up to her room and Cara isn't home yet."

Allie grabbed the plates and started setting the table. "I thought Cara had tonight off," Allie stated.

"She does," Kym replied. "She was upset about not getting to see Trent and Jenna suggested they go for a walk and talk about it."

Allie sat down at the table as Kym placed the bowl of stir fry in the center of the table. Allie scooped some up and placed it on her plate. "Well, apparently the talk didn't go so well. That's too bad but on the other hand that means there's more food for me." She took a bite and moaned, "This is so good!"

Cara walked in through the door and saw the girls eating. "This looks amazing!" she said sitting down. "I'm starving!" She scooped up a plateful of food and was about to take a bite when she noticed that the two girls were staring at her. "What?" she asked.

Kym was the first to speak, "What's going on?"

Cara looked from one girl to the other. "I'm hungry and thought I'd join you girls for dinner."

Allie shook her head. "You know what Kym's talking about. Your high pitched fake happy voice gives you away, not to mention the red splotches all over your face that tells us that you've been crying."

Cara put down her fork and sighed. "You know Jenna. She's moody. We were talking and then she just flipped out on me. You guys know how she can be. It just upset me that's all."

Allie looked at Cara skeptically. "Is there anything you want to talk about? You know we're here for you."

Cara smiled. "I know. You guys are the best. I'm fine, really. Now, can we just eat?"

Allie looked down at her plate of food, picked up her fork, took a bite and groaned. "Kym you really should become a chef. This tastes like something you would get in a gourmet restaurant and believe me I've been to plenty of those."

Kym beamed. "I'm glad you like it. The best part about this arrangement is that I can have fun and cook, and I don't have to worry about cleaning up any of the mess."

Cara looked at Allie and said, "This is totally worth us cleaning up after you."

Allie took another bite and nodded in agreement.

Chapter 9
Kym

Kym put on her running shoes and walked out the door. The fall temperatures made it perfect for running. She took a deep breath and then started out in a slow warm up. She thought about Jenna and Cara. They just haven't been themselves lately. Kym had never seen them so mad at each other and it felt really awkward when both Jenna and Cara were in the same room together. They refuse to speak to each other and ignore anything the other person is saying. It has really made living there uncomfortable.

Kym was really beginning to worry about them. Jenna spends most of her time in her room these days and lately she's been skipping classes. Cara has been quiet and glued to her phone hoping that Trent will call. She's caught her crying a few times and she knows that something is really wrong but whenever she tries talking to Cara about it she just says everything is fine and goes to her room. At first, Kym thought they just had a disagreement, but it's been going on a week and they still glare at each other and refuse to speak to one another.

Kym was glad Allie was still normal; at least there was one person in their house she could count on. Kym arrived home after her jog and saw Allie sitting at the counter working on one of her drawings. She walked over to her. "What are you working on?"

Allie looked up and said, "I'm designing a play area for kids in hospitals who are battling cancer. I want a place where they will love to be. It has to be safe of course but also liberating so that they can just be a kid you know?"

Kym looked at the bright yellow walls with big red and blue circles overlapping it. "When it comes to making the room safe you can always ask Cara. She's been working in the oncology wing lately."

Allie smiled. "That's what makes you a genius. You are full of great ideas."

Kym smiled, and her stomach growled. "I'm going to grab a shower and then make breakfast. Are you hungry?"

Allie looked at her friend. "When am I not hungry?"

Kym quickly showered and then started making breakfast. She was standing in the kitchen frying bacon when Jenna came home. "Bacon? Kym, you are the best!" she said. "I could live on bacon alone."

Kym smiled and was happy to see Jenna in a better mood as her friend grabbed a couple of pieces of bacon off of the plate. "I'm also making eggs and toast, so don't fill up."

Jenna shook her head. "This is fine, I've got a ton of studying to do."

Kym looked up. "Are you sure?"

Jenna began walking up the stairs. "I have a project due tomorrow and I haven't even started so, yes, I'm sure."

Kym turned to Allie. "I just can't figure her out. She's hardly gone to class all week and now she's worried about a project."

Allie looked up from her drawing. "I've noticed that too. I know she and Cara have been arguing but lately it seems like one minute she's in a great mood without a care in the world and then later she seems so quiet and kind of depressed. She hasn't been herself."

Cara walked into the kitchen. "What time is it?"

"Ten thirty, why?" Allie asked. "Are you going to Trent's today?" At the sound of Trent's name Allie could see she struck a nerve. "Sorry Cara. I didn't mean anything by it."

Cara shrugged and walked into the living room and turned on the television. The phone rang and Allie answered it. The phone was for Jenna. She walked towards Jenna's room and knocked on the door. "Jenna, the phone is for you." She could hear Jenna groan and walk down to answer it.

"Hi, Jenna, are you coming to class today to help present the psychology project?"

Jenna looked up at the ceiling and groaned. "That's today? I haven't even started."

The voice on the other end continued, "What do you mean you haven't started. Our grades depend on everyone presenting their part of the project. You've got to be there."

Jenna rolled her eyes. "I'll try." And she hung up and walked back to her room.

Allie and Kym looked at each other. "Maybe I should go talk to her," said Kym. "I hate seeing her this way."

Allie shook her head and went back to her drawing. Kym knocked on the door. "Jenna?"

In response Jenna threw a shoe which banged loudly against the door. "Go away! I'm sleeping."

Kym could hear Jenna crying and cautiously cracked open the door. She could see that she had been right judging from Jenna's red blotchy face and the mound of Kleenex piled up on her bed.

Kym walked in before Jenna could say or throw anything and sat on the edge of her bed. "What happened?" she asked sympathetically.

Jenna looked at Kym and then rolled her eyes towards the ceiling. "I don't know. I don't know what's wrong. I guess I'm just overwhelmed."

Kym hugged her. "It's okay, we all feel that way sometimes. You're not alone."

Jenna began again. "I feel like I'm a million miles away from everyone. I feel like I'm just going through the motions, but I'm not truly present you know?"

Kym leant against her. "Oh, Jenna, I think everyone feels that way now and again. It's called life. At least that's what my father says. I miss my family and although you guys are great I still feel lonely sometimes. It's just a bad day that's all."

Jenna wiped her eyes and blew her nose. "Then there's the argument with Cara. I can't even walk into a room without feeling like I don't belong. Maybe I should just move out."

Kym shook her head. "You do belong. We love having you here. You and Cara are just going through a rough patch. You guys will work it out."

Jenna scoffed. "I doubt that but thanks anyway. You're a good friend, Kym. Thank you for not judging me as a lazy, good for nothing person like my parents and mostly everyone else does."

Kym regarded Jenna for a minute and felt genuinely sorry for her. Her family may place a lot of expectations on her, but she never felt the way Jenna feels. Kym smiled and said, "My mother always told me that this too shall pass."

Jenna snorts out what sounds like a laugh and crawls out of bed. Kym stands up beside her. "You're already missing what sounds like an important group meeting that I bet if you hurry you can still make. Then you have an English class and I might need your help with *my* next project so get going." Kym smiles at Jenna who groans but starts to get ready.

About fifteen minutes later Jenna comes bounding down the stairs with her backpack slung over her shoulder. Kym looks over at her and sees that Jenna's makeup has covered up her splotches. Jenna grins and says, "I know, Mom, I'm going to be late for class." She comes over and gives Kym a hug before she leaves. "Thank you," she whispers.

It's nice to feel needed Kym thinks to herself as she sits down on the sofa and picks up the television remote. She flips to the Hallmark channel and immediately hears Cara and Allie groan.

"Romance is overrated," Allie complains, and Cara backs her up by saying, "Guys are jerks. Don't fall for their charm."

Kym turns up the volume and says, "I disagree."

Allie pulls on her coat. "I'm going out for some ice cream." She looks at Cara and Kym. "Do you girls want to come along?" Cara readily jumps at her invitation, but Kym shakes her head no. The two girls leave as Kym settles in with a hot cup of tea and a blanket thrown around her. She stretches out contentedly on the couch; *I have no classes for the rest of the day and I have the whole house to myself.*

Kym jumped when the phone rang. "Hello?"

"Kym, I'm so glad you are home. It's your father..."

"Mom, slow down. I can't understand you."

"Kym, your father..." she choked back a sob. "He's at the hospital."

"Oh. My. God! What happened? Is he going to be okay?"

"I don't know yet. The doctors are with him now. Honey, they say he had a heart attack."

Kym stood up pacing back and forth feeling panicked and helpless. Tears were flowing freely down her face. "I'm coming home. I'll be on the next flight back to Hong Kong." The phone is quiet. "Hello? Mom are you still there?"

"I'm here," she says in a whisper. "Don't come. It's expensive and you know your father. If he finds out that I called and distracted you from your studies he'd be furious with me. I will call later and let you know how he's doing."

"What? No! I'm coming home. Mom..." Kym looked incredulously at the phone as the dial tone echoed in her ear. She hung up and wiped at the tears that refused to stop falling. How can this be happening? Her father was the strongest man she knew. She couldn't imagine her life without him. She felt so helpless. She wiped away her tears and logged onto her computer and looked up the price of a plane ticket. She had never gone against her parents' wishes before but this was the exception. She couldn't just sit by and do nothing. Her heart sank when she saw that the price of a plane ticket was $1,500. She had nothing near that amount of money. She wiped away her tears that were continuing to fall as anger welled up inside her.

She picked up the phone again to call her mother. She held the receiver in her hand and started dialing the number then hurled it across the room hitting a wall and breaking it into pieces. She had to get out of here. The silence was deafening. She opened the front door and started to run. She ran and ran and ran as her anger continued to build higher and higher, fueling her to run faster.

She thought of her father lying helplessly in a hospital bed and her mother sitting alone in the waiting room. She felt as though she would burst with anger as she replayed her mother's words over and over. The realization of her mother's words kept ringing in her ears, *Don't come. If he finds out that I called and distracted you from your studies he'd be furious with me.* She ran faster in disbelief that they expected her to stay here and continue her studies. Really? The part that pisses her off the most is that she will do it. She will stay and be the dutiful daughter that they've groomed her to be. She stopped in her tracks and wiped at the tears that refused to stop running down her face. Kym felt so tired, so defeated. She just wanted to be herself. She just wanted to be home. Instead, she was left with the dismal reality that her parents are counting on her to bring them to America. She is the only person who will either epically fail or make ***their*** dreams come true.

Chapter 10
Girls Night Out

Allie and Cara came bounding through the door soaking wet from the pouring rain that popped up out of nowhere. The house was silent, and all of the lights were off. "Kym!" Allie yelled as she went to grab a towel to dry off. "Are you home?"

"Do you see a note? Cara asked drying her hair with a towel.

Allie looked around, "Nope, maybe she got tired of watching sappy romance movies. But it's not like her to just take off like this."

Cara frowned when she saw the phone in pieces scattered along the living room floor, "What happened? This definitely isn't like her. What is going on?"

Cara's phone rang, and she pulled it out of her back pocket and looked at the screen. Allie could tell by the big grin on Cara's face that it was Trent. She could also tell that Cara was wavering between answering it or sending him to voicemail. "Go ahead and answer it Cara. I'll try and call Kym on her cell phone to make sure she's okay."

Cara answered her phone, "Hi handsome. It's about time you called me back." Allie could tell when Cara's face slowly changed from radiant to crestfallen that it wasn't good news. "But Trent it's been three long weeks." There was silence again as she heard Cara whisper in a lower voice, "I'm not whining I just miss you. I hate not seeing you and we barely talk anymore."

Allie walked into the kitchen to give Cara some privacy. It wasn't long before Cara stomped angrily into the kitchen and tossed her phone on the counter. She sat on a stool and glared at the phone.

"I take it Trent's having a bad day?" Allie asked.

Cara scoffed. "He's having a bad day? I wouldn't know, he never stays on the phone long enough for me to find out. He's not even a doctor yet and all I hear is I have to go. Talk later. Hell, he doesn't even tell me he loves me anymore."

"He's probably just busy. No worries," Allie said encouragingly.

"You're probably right. It just gets frustrating sometimes you know?" Cara looks at Allie and said, "You are smart not to have a long-distance relationship."

Allie laughed and replied, "That's where you're mistaken my friend, I am smart because I refuse to have a relationship at all. Who's to say there's only one person for each of us? There's too much of the world I want to see and experience. Being tied down in one place with one person would make me miserable."

Allie reached into the freezer and pulled out a container of mint chocolate chip ice cream and two spoons. She handed one to Cara. Cara let out a long sigh and took the spoon. She plunked a spoonful of ice cream into her mouth and rolled her eyes. "Allie, you missed your calling. You should have been a shrink. Ice cream fixes everything. By the way did you get a hold of Kym?"

Allie shook her head. "Nope, I called just to discover that her phone is on the coffee table. I hope everything is okay."

They were lost in their own thoughts as Jenna walked through the front door lugging her heavy backpack and dropped it on the floor. She turned and slammed the door, glared at the two girls eating ice cream and quickly stomped up to her room with her head down. "I guess I'm not the only one having a tough day," muttered Cara.

She scooped up another spoonful of ice cream. "I wonder what's got her so riled up."

Allie stopped her. "Cara, I know you two aren't getting along but you both need to give each other a break and talk this thing through."

Cara thought for a minute and picked her spoon back up. "Yeah, I guess you're right. Maybe I'll let her apologize since I've done nothing wrong, and the way I see it she has a lot to apologize for."

Allie rolled her eyes and looked in the direction that Jenna had walked. "I am starting to worry about her," she stated.

"Jenna? Why?"

Allie replied, "She's just not herself. She's been really moody lately haven't you noticed? Take today for example, everyone has bad days, but do you come home and drop your stuff on the floor then turn around and slam the door? Plus, who stomps up the stairs? Three-year-olds, that's who. It's just not normal. Lately, she's been spending so much time in her room blaring her head banging music that sometimes I have to leave the house just to find some peace and quiet." Allie shakes her head. "Sometimes, I don't think she even bothers going to class by the looks of her when I get home. Instead it looks like she just woke up and dragged herself out of bed and it'll be three in the afternoon." Allie ate another spoonful of ice cream and said. "Maybe she's depressed or something."

Cara thought about Jenna and tried to put their argument aside to analyze the situation from a medical perspective. "Maybe you're right Allie. Maybe something is going on with her. I'm not convinced she's depressed but she's definitely not the same person who moved in here at the beginning of the month."

Cara thought about Jenna confessing about the conversations she had been having with Jeff and she could see that Jenna had feelings for him whether Jenna wanted to admit it or not. She hadn't said anything to Allie yet and was debating on doing so. Cara tucked those thoughts in the back of her mind and lied. "Maybe something is just bothering her like one of her classes or maybe her parents."

Cara continued thinking out loud. "During the past few weeks I have noticed that she spends a lot of time in her room, but I didn't think much about it. I noticed she missed a few classes but figured that's just Jenna and she was in a mood."

They continued to eat their ice cream in silence when Kym came bounding in through the door. She was soaked in sweat mixed with rain and her hair fell limp around her face. She looked awful. She still couldn't stop the tears from pouring down her face. She just stood there looking at them and crying.

"Kym, what's wrong? Are you okay?" Cara asked as she went over and led Kym towards the chair. Kym shook her head no and shakily sat down. Cara grabbed a blanket and wrapped it around Kym's shoulders. Allie grabbed another spoon and handed it to Kym. Kym let out a little smile but didn't take it.

It took Kym a few minutes to compose herself. She looked at her two friends, her American family. "It's my father..." She gulped for air and tried to slow her racing heart. Saying the words were so hard, "...he had a heart attack."

Allie looked at her friend. "Oh my god! You need to get home!" Allie walked over and hugged Kym.

Cara immediately grabbed her purse and keys. "We'll drive you to the airport."

Kym shook her head back and forth and cried harder although she didn't know how she could have any tears left. "I'm not going," she choked. "My mother said... she said... I have to stay here. I need to continue my studies. She said that my father would be angry if he knew I flew home."

Allie looked at Cara then back to Kym. "Why would your father be angry? I'm sure he would understand why you felt you had to go home to see him."

Kym shook her head. "You do not understand. My family, they are different than American family. I have to do well and get my citizenship so that they can move here. I cannot disappoint them."

Allie put her arm around Kym's shoulders. "I am so sorry. I'm sure your dad will be okay." Allie looked at Cara questioningly.

Cara came over and hugged them both. "Of course he will. Medical technology has come a long way. I'm sure your father will be just fine and he's getting the best care."

Allie stood up and let out a long breath. "Wow, it's been a terrible day for everyone. I say we walk down to Mulcahey's Pub and have a beer. Maybe getting out of the house will be good for everyone."

Cara looked at Allie and smiled sadly. "I second that." She looked sympathetically at Kym. "Go take a shower and freshen up and we'll get out of here for a while. It'll help take our minds off things and when we come back we'll call and see how your dad is doing. It'll be awhile before the doctors are finished with all of their tests. In the meantime, it will be a good distraction." Kym got up and began walking shakily up the stairs towards the shower.

Allie looked at Cara warningly and then walked over and shouted up the stairs, "Jenna you're going with us to Mulcahey's. You have half an hour to be dressed and ready."

Half an hour later all four girls were heading out the door. Kym and Jenna were still solemn as they walked behind Allie and Cara along the sidewalk leading to the pub. It was a clear night and all the stars were out. The moon was full overhead, lighting the way.

The girls could hear the jukebox blaring before they ever reached their destination. The parking lot was crowded as they weaved through cars to make their way to the door. Allie opened the door as her friends piled in. Jenna immediately began to relax. There was something about the atmosphere of a bar that relaxed her. Maybe it was the music blaring through the jukebox or just being surrounded by friends and forgetting about life for a while. The bar was even more crowded than the parking lot as the girls wove through people and settled on a booth near a window.

Allie waved to someone on the dance floor then she and Cara walked up to the bar to order a round of drinks. Jenna studied Kym looking concerned. “I’m sorry about your dad. Is there anything I can do to help?”

Kym’s eyes started tearing up again and she shook her head no. Jenna was about to speak again when Allie arrived at the table. “Here you go ladies,” she announced proudly as she carried four beers on a round tray and Cara followed behind carrying 4 shots of tequila.

Jenna lifted a wary eye at Cara who said, “It’s been a bad day and I think that we could all use this right now.”

Jenna smiled. Kym reached for a beer and started to drink. She looked skeptically at Cara and said, “You know I don’t do shots. You can have mine.”

“Oh, no you don’t,” Cara ordered. “If anyone needs a shot after today it’s you.”

Allie held up her shot glass. “Let’s make a toast.”

All four girls held up their glasses. “To a better tomorrow.” They all clinked glasses, tossed back their tequila, sucked their lemon wedge, and took another gulp of beer.

It was noisy in the bar, loud enough to chase away the demons but comforting enough to sit back and relax. Allie glanced at the crowd and waved to some friends who were out on the dance floor. They beckoned her to come over. “Be right back,” she said sliding out of the booth. Kym looked down at her empty beer glass and began feeling the effects of the alcohol starting to relax her. She stood up and walked to the bar to get a refill.

Cara looked at Jenna who was still sitting quietly bobbing her head to the music. “Kym told me about this morning,” Cara said. Jenna looked at her in surprise as Cara continued, “We’re all worried about you.”

Jenna shrugged her shoulders and said, “There’s nothing to worry about. It was just a bad day, and everyone has them. I’m probably just going through a phase. That’s what my parents always said anyway.”

Cara shook her head. “I’m not so sure Jenna. You’ve been moody as hell. One minute you’re happy and fun and the next minute you hate the world and everyone in it. I just think that something more may be going on. We care about you and we want to see you happy. I know a great doctor you could see.”

Jenna turned her head to look around the bar to avoid her friend's eyes. "Really, Cara, it's nothing. I'm sure it'll pass. Let's just drop it okay?"

"Jenna, I'm a nursing student. I know when there's more than meets the eye. I care about you. You're my best friend. Please, please get help. I hate seeing you like this."

Jenna's eyes began tearing up and she wiped them away quickly hoping no one would notice. "I'm not so sure we are friends," Jenna replied.

Cara sighed and said, "Of course we're friends. We both said a lot of hurtful things. I know I'm not proud of what I said."

Jenna took a shaky breath. "Neither am I. I was just hurt, and I turned my anger on you. I meant what I said about not trusting Trent, but I shouldn't have said it the way that I did and I'm sorry."

Cara held up her glass in a toast. "To new beginnings?" she asked.

Jenna clinked her glass against Cara's. "To new beginnings."

"So back to what I was saying about you seeing this great doctor... He's very nice looking and if nothing else you would have eye candy for the day."

Jenna smiled and said resignedly, "Fine, Mom. I'll go see the doctor but I'm telling you it's nothing."

Cara looked at her smiling. "Thank you."

Kym came back carrying another round of beers. "Whoa," said Cara looking at her half-filled glass. "I'd better catch up." She finished her drink and reached for another on the table.

Jenna looked at Kym and said, "You might want to slow down a little or you won't make it until closing time."

Kym looked at her friend and said, "That's the point. I want to drink until I pass out and forget this day ever happened."

Cara reached across the table to clink her glass against Kym's. "Me too," she said.

Jenna looked over at Cara and said, "Let me guess. Trent's a jerk."

Cara shrugged her shoulders and took another sip. "When isn't he these days?"

Jenna knew better than to say anything else about the subject. She cared too much about her friend, plus what did Jenna know? She had never been in a serious relationship and after seeing what Cara was going through she didn't plan on having one for a very long time. Allie walked back over to their table and grabbed Cara and Kym's hand while looking at Jenna. "Come on ladies let's dance."

All four of them stayed on the dance floor for most of the night. Allie made sure the jukebox stayed stacked full with all of their favorites. This is what life is about, Allie thought, watching her friends dancing. It's about good times, laughter, and letting it all go. Allie joined them back out on the dance floor and swayed to the music. There was something about music that had always soothed her soul. She laughed when some of her friends came over to join them. By the end of the night everyone was dancing like no one was watching. There was an intoxicating energy in the air filled with laughter, flirting, and drinking until closing time.

Chapter 11
Trent's House

Jenna looked at her watch and hurriedly walked towards her pre-law class. She was excited to finally be starting a class in her major instead of only general education classes. Her phone rang and she looked at the caller id. It was Cara. "Hi Cara, what's up?

"I was calling to see how your appointment went."

Jenna smiled and thought how she will forever be grateful to Cara for suggesting that she see someone about her mood swings. "Everything is good. My meds are working like they should, and I can't remember feeling this good. I'm on my way to class now and I don't want to be late. I'll fill you in when I get home."

"Okay, see ya," Cara said. She hung up the phone and smiled. She was glad she could help Jenna. In the last few months Jenna seemed like a different person. Once she got her bi-polar disorder under control she was laughing and more active instead of sitting in her room every day. Cara walked into the kitchen and looked at the clock. Trent should be home by now. She picked up her phone and dialed his number. He answered on the second ring, "Hey, can I call you back? I'm at the hospital."

"Sure," Cara replied. "I love you."

"Me too," he said hurriedly and hung up.

Cara plopped her phone on the counter. She could already feel her good mood dissipating. She thought back to the last time they had finally seen each other. She could sense things were changing between them. Now their conversations revolved around work and classes instead of their future. She knew they had a long way to go before they could start planning a wedding, buying a house, and starting their family. More than anything she missed ***them*** and, as much as she hated to admit it, Jenna's remark about him cheating on her was always in the back of her mind.

She walked over to the freezer and took out a quart of chocolate ice cream and a spoon. Kym came in through the doorway breathless and trying to sound calm. She had her phone to her ear. "Mother please stop crying. What is it? Is it father?"

She looked at Cara who turned and grabbed another spoon. Kym listened to her mother. "Kym, your father had been doing so well since the surgery. Your aunt and I have been working at the market so that he could rest. He was making great progress and feeling better since he came home."

Cara handed her a spoon. Kym interrupted, "Was?"

Her mother started crying again. "He had another heart attack."

Kym looked at Cara, her eyes filling with tears. "Is he going to be okay?"

"He died, honey."

Kym dropped the spoon and cried out in anguish.

Cara reached over and grabbed the phone from Kym. "Hello? Mrs. Syndako? Are you there?"

Cara could hear sobbing on the other end of the line. "Mrs. Syndako, its Cara, Kym's roommate."

She put an arm around Kym and was rubbing her arm up and down. Cara listened intently on the line, her eyes tearing up as she began to understand what was going on. "I'll make sure she's on the next plane home."

Kym caught her breath. *Was her mother really going to allow her to come home?*

Cara stopped speaking as it was evident that her mother was interrupting. "But Mrs. Syndako, Kym needs to be home. She needs to say goodbye. She needs to be with her family. Hello? Hello?" Cara looked at the phone.

She looked down at Kym. "We must have gotten disconnected."

"She hung up on you. She told me not to come."

"I don't understand," Cara said gently.

Kym took a deep breath and tried to speak through her sobs. "My family is counting on me. I will not disrespect my father's memory. I have to stay."

Cara stands up in outrage. "That's ridiculous! You need to be home with your family."

Kym sadly shook her head. "No, I need to honor my father's wishes."

Cara opened her mouth to say something as the front door opened and Allie walked through the door. She looked at both of her friends' tear stained cheeks and asked, "What happened?"

Kym wiped her face and looked at Allie. "Is it your dad?" Allie asked. Kym nodded her head, yes. Allie came over to hug her. "Is he okay?" Kym shook her head no and got up and walked briskly to her room and slammed the door.

Allie looked at Cara, "What happened?"

Cara replied still in shock, "Kym's father had another heart attack and died."

"Oh wow! We've got to get her to the airport," Allie exclaimed.

Cara shook her head. "We can't. Her mother doesn't want her to come. Kym kept saying she can't disappoint her family. She has to stay here."

"Wow! Poor Kym," Allie said.

Allie walked into the kitchen and looked at the ice cream sitting on the counter. It was partially melted. "That kind of a day, huh?"

Cara tried to muster a smile. "Yeah, that kind of a day. Trent... need I say more?"

Allie shook her head. "No words needed my friend. No words needed."

Allie put the ice cream in the freezer and picked up the phone. She looked at Cara. "Should I order in tonight? There's not much in the cupboards and I'm not in the mood to make dinner." Cara nodded, and Allie pushed speed dial for Tony's Pizza Hut.

Jenna walked in the house and saw Allie pulling out plates and Cara grabbing some beer out of the refrigerator. "Pizza and beer? My day just got better." Jenna dropped her bag on the couch and took off her coat. "Where's Kym?" she asked.

Cara quietly explained to Jenna what had happened. Jenna picked up two beers and walked towards Kym's room. She quickly rapped on the door and opened it. "Hey, Kym," Jenna said sympathetically as she walked towards her bed.

Kym scooted over as Jenna climbed in beside her. "I'm sorry about your dad." Jenna handed her a beer.

Kym took a swig and then leaned her head back against the headboard. "I can't believe my mother won't let me come home."

Jenna was quiet for a minute and said, "Yeah, that's messed up." The two girls sat in silence and sipped their beer. Jenna said, "I know we're not your real family but we're here for you. You know that right?"

Kym wiped back the tears trickling down her face. "I know. It's just hard. He was my dad you know?"

Jenna took a swig of beer. "I know. You were lucky to have a dad. I just had a man living in a house who I called Dad. He never really spent much time with me. Mainly he just judged me, and I never measured up."

Kym looked at Jenna. "That's sad."

Jenna blew out a breath, she was never good at discussing her personal feelings with people. "Yeah it is."

There was a rap on the door and Allie came in carrying a pizza box. "Can we join you guys?" Cara asked hopefully.

"Of course, you can," Kym said sadly. "I need my family around me. You guys are my family."

Everyone sat on Kym's bed and listened to her tell stories about her dad. Sometimes they laughed and other times they cried. But they were together and that's all that mattered.

Allie explained to Kym that there were many ways people chose to say goodbye to a loved one. Some people chose to do a memorial and celebrate their loved one's life while others mourned quietly. Kym liked the idea of celebrating her father's life.

"Would you like to walk down to Mulcahey's Pub and celebrate your dad?" Allie asked gently

Kym looked down at her hands trying to hold back the tears that were threatening to fall again.

"Come on," Cara said pulling her friend from the bed. "It might help being around people."

Kym wiped away a tear and drew in a shaky breath. "Maybe you're right," she said.

All four girls stood up and walked down the hall. They slipped on their jackets and walked out into the cool crisp air. Kym looked up at all the stars. She hoped she'd make her father proud. She knew it was up to her to bring her mother here and she wouldn't disappoint him. The girls linked arms together as they walked in silence each in their own thoughts.

Mulcahey's Pub was quieter tonight. The dim lights and the melancholy music coming from the jukebox matched the girls' moods. They grabbed a booth then Cara and Jenna went to grab drinks from the bar. Jenna carried over 4 beers while Cara came over carrying a tray toting four shots of tequila. She handed a shot glass to each girl.

"I propose a toast," Allie said holding up her glass. "To Mr. Syndako, a great man who raised a great girl who I'm proud to say is one of my best friends."

"Hear, hear," Jenna replied.

They clinked glasses and tossed back their drinks. Kym felt the burning liquid slide down her throat and she was thankfully beginning to feel numb. She still couldn't believe her father was gone.

Cara looked at her phone and frowned. She'd been waiting for Trent to call. He had to be home by now. She hadn't seen him in weeks and lately they've been playing phone tag. She tried calling him again. "Hello, you've reached Trent Avery. You know what to do." BEEP. Cara hung up. She'd already left two messages, but he hadn't called back. She finished off her beer and walked up to the bar and ordered another shot. *Eventually, he'll call back* she thought.

Jenna felt sympathetic as she watched Cara. She wouldn't bring their argument up again, but she didn't trust Trent. He had an arrogance about him and no doubt a roaming eye. Jenna knew his kind well. She walked up to Cara. "Trouble in paradise?"

Cara laughed bitterly. "I feel like I'm in high school again. I'm this insecure girl waiting for a guy to call her. How pathetic."

Jenna ordered another shot for her friend. "That is pathetic," Jenna agreed.

Cara looked at her incredulously and then burst out laughing. "So much for your bedside manner," Cara said.

Jenna laughed. "You're too good for him. You deserve better."

"You're right," Cara agreed. "But I love him." She took another sip of her beer and looked at Jenna. "Do you think he's cheating on me?"

Jenna sighed. "I don't know Cara. It's possible. He went from calling you at least three times a day to like three times a week. But then again he might just be busy like he says."

Cara motions to the bartender for another shot. She looked at Jenna. "I've got to know. This is making me crazy."

Jenna choked on her drink. "Now?"

"Yes, now. I can't keep going on like this."

Jenna put down her beer. "Well... I haven't drunk as much as you. I guess I can drive. Are you sure?"

Cara hesitated and then said, "Yes, I'm sure. Let's go."

The girls stood up to leave and Allie shouted across the room. "Wait a minute you two. Where do you think you're going without us?"

Jenna looked at Cara who shrugged her shoulders giving her the go ahead. Kym looked the most intoxicated with Cara coming in a close second. They waited while Kym and

Allie caught up. They walked back to the house as Jenna filled them in. The three girls waited by the car as Jenna ran in and grabbed her keys. She climbed behind the wheel as Cara sat shotgun beside her so that she could give directions. It wasn't too long after they left that Kym passed out in the back seat. Allie closed her eyes and relaxed as Cara and Jenna talked.

Two hours later they turned off the lights and pulled up silently in front of Trent's house behind his blaze orange mustang, a graduation gift from his parents. Cara let out a nervous breath and looked at Jenna.

"I'm going with you," Jenna stated in a tone that left no argument.

Cara nodded and opened her door. Jenna followed as Cara slid her hand along the top of the doorway and produced the spare key. She silently slid the key in the lock and turned the knob. Jenna put her finger to her lips motioning for her to stay quiet as they walked in. Cara knew the layout of the house like the back of her hand. She easily made her way through the living room, down the long hallway, and stood in front of his bedroom. It was quiet. *That's a good sign.* She looked at Jenna. She was having second thoughts.

"Maybe this was a bad idea," Cara whispered. "It doesn't look like anyone else is here. I don't want to wake him, and he'd probably be pissed if he knew I was checking up on him."

Jenna shook her head. "I did not just drive two hours for you to chicken out now. Just open the door and look. If he's sleeping alone then we'll leave, and he'll never know."

Cara shook her head in agreement and tried to gather her resolve that was beginning to wane. "You're right. Just a quick peek, that's all." She put her hand on the doorknob and turned. She looked in. It was dark, and she could barely make out Trent sleeping in bed. "It's just him," she exhaled in relief.

Jenna pushed the door open a little wider. The door to the adjoining bathroom swung open and a slim, naked, female body stepped into the bedroom. The unidentified female looked towards the open doorway and screamed. Trent bolted upright and turned on the lamp next to his bed. His eyes were still trying to focus as Jenna came bolting through the door. "You son of a bitch! How could you do this to her!"

Cara caught up to her friend. She was still in shock. She looked at Trent and then at the breathtaking blonde with blue eyes and flowing long hair. She looked like a model. Cara felt sick. She ran towards the bathroom as the pizza roiling in her stomach began to churn. Jenna jumped on the bed and started hitting Trent. "You son of a bitch!" she yelled again.

The blonde spoke, "Trent, what is going on? Who are *they*?"

Trent pushed Jenna off of him and jumped out of bed. He headed towards the bathroom. "Cara, it's not what it looks like."

Cara puked again and then shouted, "Oh really? Because it looks to me that it is exactly what it looks like."

The blonde followed Trent towards the bathroom. "Trent, I thought you told me that you weren't in a relationship. You said you were falling for me."

Trent turned and looked at her like it was the first time. "Not now," he ordered.

The blonde walked over to the pile of clothes on the floor and quickly got dressed. Then she sexily sauntered back over to him dressed in a very low scooped teal shirt that showed her voluptuous breasts and a short black mini-skirt. She took his face in both of her hands and turned him towards her. She leaned in and gave him a long deep kiss as Cara and Jenna looked incredulously at them then she patted his cheek. "Not ever, sweetheart."

She slipped on her three-inch heels and looked sadly at Cara. "I'm sorry. I didn't know."

Cara looked up at her and then turned her head and puked again.

Trent ran his fingers through his short blonde hair. He grimaced and leaned back against the wall. "Cara, we need to talk."

She stood up and wiped her mouth with the back of her hand. "We need to talk NOW? I've been calling you for THREE WEEKS and NOW you want to talk?"

She walked over to him with her arms flailing but Jenna interceded. "Come on, Cara. Let's go. You're wasting your breath on this loser."

Cara stood in front of Trent. "You arrogant piece of shit. You told me you loved me. You told me you missed me. You told me we were going to have a life together." She ran her hand across her nose as the tears started spilling. "This was our first time apart and you just couldn't keep your dick in your pants. *Really?*"

She looked at Jenna and said, "You're right. We're done here." She slid the ring that Trent gave her off of her finger and threw it at him then she stormed out of the house. She walked straight towards the car without a backwards glance and climbed into the driver's seat.

Jenna caught up to her. "Cara, get out. I'm driving."

Cara laughed bitterly. "I'm fine. I've puked, and I've just ended my relationship. I'm sober, believe me."

The engine roared to life as Cara put the car in reverse. Jenna ran over to the passenger side door and jumped in.

Chapter 12
March 25, 2016

Everyone sat in silence as Cara sped out of the driveway and down the road. Once we were out of city limits Cara started to speak. "Stupid! Stupid! Stupid! I was so stupid!" She was crying harder and then hit the steering wheel.

Jenna spoke, "He's an asshole. You're better off without him."

Cara leaned her head back against the seat trying to catch her breath, her tears flowing down her face. "You know what the ironic part is?" Cara sobbed. "He's cheated on me before and like an idiot I forgave him. I'm so stupid!" Cara quickly swerved to the side of the road and stopped. She opened the door and jumped out just as she started to puke again.

Allie got out of the car and knelt down next to Cara. Allie rubbed Cara's back and was talking soothingly to her. Jenna leaned over and turned off the car and pocketed the keys. She opened the door and got out. It was so peaceful and quiet out here. No bright lights. No sirens. Just welcoming silence.

Once Cara had calmed down she looked up at Jenna and said, "I was wrong. You have the better end of the deal."

Jenna looked at Cara confused. "What are you talking about?"

Cara laughed sarcastically. "Being the other girl, the one that guys cheat on with." Jenna thought she would die.

Allie looked at Jenna confused. "What is she talking about?"

Cara looked at Allie. "She never told you?"

Allie looked back at Jenna. "Told me what?"

Cara shook her head in disbelief and then puked again.

Allie looked at Jenna and said, "What do you have to tell me?"

Before Jenna had the chance to answer Allie's phone rang. She answered it and smiled. She heard Jeff's deep voice whisper in her ear, "Hi sweetheart. I miss you."

Allie smiled in spite of herself. "You've been drinking haven't you."

Jeff laughed, "Maybe just a little. When can we get together? I miss you." Allie looked at the girls and asked, "Where are we?"

Jenna replied, "Near Syracuse."

Allie smiled and spoke into the phone, "How about in half an hour at Mickey's Hideout."

Jeff shouted, and Allie had to hold the phone away from her ear. She laughed and hung up. She took the keys from Jenna and said, "How about a little detour girls?"

Kym looked at Allie skeptically. “Detour to where?”

Allie smiled. “We’re close to Syracuse and Jeff and his friends are at Mickey’s Hideout. We’re going to meet up with them.”

Jenna’s heart fluttered. She and Jeff had been texting each other constantly and their conversations had gotten more serious. She was starting to have feelings for him and the way he was flirting with her made her think he had feelings for her too. They had talked about meeting up, but they hadn’t had the chance. She didn’t want to sneak around behind Allie’s back but she didn’t want to say anything to Allie until she knew for sure where she and Jeff stood.

Kym looked at Cara. “I don’t think that’s a good idea. Cara seems pretty sick and it’s getting late.”

Allie’s face looked crestfallen and was quiet for a minute. “Okay, how about you drop me off at Mickey’s and then I’ll find a way home later.”

Cara shook her head. “I’m okay. I’m with Allie. Let’s go and have a little fun. It’s been a depressing night and I can use the distraction.”

Kym looked at Jenna who shrugged her shoulders. They piled back into the car as Allie sped off towards Mickey’s.

Jenna sat in the back of the car., She excitedly pulled out her phone and texted Jeff.

Jenna: Hi handsome, I can’t wait to see you!

Jeff: I miss you too. One of these days we’ll meet up.

Jenna: How about tonight?

Jeff: Sorry I have plans.

Jenna: I know. I’m with Allie and we’re on our way :)

Jenna waited for Jeff's reply, but one didn't come. *Maybe he got distracted?*

Jenna: Are you there?

Jeff: Yes, still here. Who is coming with Allie?

Jenna: Me, Cara, and Kym

Jeff: Great! I'll call some of the guys and have them come down too.

Thirty minutes later Allie pulled into a crowded parking lot at the bar. The girls quickly glanced in the car mirror and saw that each one of them looked like they had been through hell. Jenna wanted to look her best for Jeff, so she quickly brushed her hair, wiped away her mascara smudges, and put on fresh lipstick. Allie opened her door just as Jeff came strutting out. His whole face lit up when he saw Allie. Jenna felt her heart sink looking at him. She was good at hiding her feelings and she made sure she hid them well. She thought back to all the times they talked on the phone. The times she was beginning to open up to him. The times he called just to tell her she was beautiful.

She watched as his arms wrapped around Allie's body and how Allie leaned in to give him a kiss. Jeff looked up and saw the rest of the girls standing next to the car. He slowly let go and walked over to Jenna. "Hi, Jenna." He leaned in for a hug, but it felt awkward as Jenna returned it. He looked at her quizzically and then walked over and pulled Cara and Kym into a group hug. He kept his arms around them and said, "Come on ladies. Let's get this party started."

They all walked into the bar together and made a beeline towards the bar. Jeff ordered everyone a round of drinks. Jenna smiled and looked at Jeff hoping they could talk but he only had eyes for Allie. He whispered something in Allie's ear that made her laugh and she put her beer down while he led her to the dance floor.

Cara sat down next to Jenna. "I guess you were right."

Jenna broke her stare away from the cozy couple. "Right about what?"

Cara nodded her head towards the dance floor. "About you and Jeff only being friends. I'm sorry I didn't believe you."

Jenna shrugged nonchalantly trying to mask her disappointment. "That's okay. No big deal."

Cara took another drink. "I've decided I'm going to be more like you. I'm going to forget Trent and just have fun with no strings attached. Maybe I'll be the 'other' girl instead of the girlfriend."

Jenna looked at her friend sadly. "Don't be. You're better than me Cara. You deserve a great guy who will treat you with respect. You deserve someone who will remember your name the next day and will only have eyes for you." Jenna looked past Cara to Jeff who was pulling Allie closer to him and they danced like no one else was in the room.

Cara looked at her friend. "You really like him don't you?"

Jenna looked at Cara in surprise. "Who? Jeff? He's nice and all but definitely not my type."

Cara studied her friend. "Jenna, it's me your best friend, remember? You might not be able to open up to many people but you can trust me. I know you and I know that you're hurting right now."

Jenna took another sip of her beer and tried to mask the turmoil roiling up inside her.

Cara felt a tap on her shoulder and turned around to see a tall man with kind eyes looking at her. "Would you like to dance?" he asked.

Jenna looked at him skeptically knowing her friend was still reeling from Trent, but she couldn't help noticing his nice fitting jeans and t-shirt that accentuated his muscular frame. Most of all Jenna noticed his smile and could see he wasn't arrogant or even intoxicated instead he seemed hesitant and hopeful.

Cara replied, "No thank you. I'm talking to my friend."

Jenna smiled and looked up at the guy. "Go ahead. Take her dancing. She's a great dancer but if you hurt her or offend her in any way you will have to deal with me."

The man looked at Jenna and he could see that she was serious. "Don't worry. I will be on my best behavior."

Cara laughed and looked at Jenna who nodded for her to go with him.

Kym sat down next to Jenna and looked over at Cara dancing. "It's nice to see her smiling. I haven't seen her smile in weeks."

Jenna looked up at Kym. "I'm sorry going out and celebrating your dad's memory didn't go quite as planned."

Kym shrugged. "Nothing ever goes as planned. I'm learning that the hard way."

Jenna got the bartender's attention and ordered them each a shot. Kym seemed hesitant but took it. Jenna raised her glass in a toast. "To Mr. Syndako, may you smile down upon your daughter each and every day."

Kym's eyes welled with tears. "I don't know if I can do this."

Jenna looked at her in confusion. "Do what?"

Kym put her glass down untouched. "Obey my father's wishes. What if I fail?"

Jenna looked at her friend with concern. "You're not going to fail. You're the smartest person I know."

Kym brushed away a tear. "That's what everyone says but I'm afraid. It's only my mother and I now and we're so far away from each other."

Jenna picked up Kym's shot and drank it and sat the glass down. "Kym, if you didn't have to support anyone else. If it were just you and you alone, what would you do?"

Kym smiled ruefully. "I would cook in my own restaurant. I wouldn't want it too big but just big enough, you know?"

Jenna nodded. "Then you should do that. Do what makes you happy. I know your dad placed expectations on you but that's because he had faith in you. He was proud of you. He would want you to follow your dreams. I truly believe that."

Kym shook her head in disagreement. "My father would want me to continue with their plan."

Jenna put down her glass and looked at Kym earnestly. “Your father would want you to be happy. You could easily have a double major by majoring in culinary and in business. You could send for your mom who would already have a job in America working for you, and you could both be together.”

Kym thought about this for a while and Jenna could swear she could see a huge weight being lifted off of Kym’s shoulders. She hugged Jenna tightly. “Thank you!”

Allie and Jeff were cozied up in a booth. Allie was laughing at something Jeff said and he was leaning in closer and giving her a gentle kiss. Jenna rolled her eyes and ordered another drink. She knew she had to stop drinking. She wasn’t really supposed to mix alcohol with her medication, but right now it was the only thing that was going to get her over seeing Jeff with Allie. She was glad that Allie was happy, and she would never cross that line if Allie were truly pursuing a relationship with Jeff.

If one didn’t know better you would think they were already in a relationship, but Allie kept insisting they are just friends. If only Allie could see her face would she know that she was totally and completely in love with Jeff.

Allie caught Jenna looking at them and motioned her to come over. Her heart sank at the idea of sitting across from the happy couple. Jenna shook her head no and pointed to the shot in her hand. Allie got up and led her to the table and Jenna had no choice but to go. She shifted uncomfortably in the booth while Allie and Jeff did most of the talking. “Is something wrong? Allie asked looking at her friend.

Jenna shook her head refusing to look at Jeff. "No, I'm just tired. It's been a crazy night and it's just catching up with me."

Allie shook her head in agreement. "It's been insane."

Jeff turned the conversation back to a lighter subject by telling a joke which made everyone burst out in laughter, even Jenna.

A love song began to play, and Jeff took Allie's hand and pulled her out onto the dance floor. Allie looked at Jenna helplessly, but Jenna motioned for her to go have fun. Jenna watched them dancing closely and walked back to the bar and ordered another drink. Jenna looked around and saw that Cara was sitting at the end of the bar laughing at something the cute guy was saying. Jeff and Allie were back in their own world and Kym was talking to Jamal who was listening intently to her describing her restaurant.

Jenna reached into her purse and felt something odd. She pulled it out and remembered that Cara had tucked her cigarettes into Jenna's purse. She didn't smoke, but Cara claimed it helped with stress so why not? She walked out the door and pulled a cigarette out of the pack. She stood there feeling for a lighter but didn't find one. A couple standing close to each other were laughing and smoking. Jenna walked up to them, "Hey, can I get a light?"

"Sure," replied the guy as the girl was looking Jenna up and down wondering if she'd be competition.

It was colder now, and she was shivering. Jenna pulled a drag off of the cigarette. She looked at the girl and then at the guy. "Thanks," she said and walked off making sure all eyes were on her. She shivered in the cold sitting on a picnic table thinking of Allie and Jeff. She didn't want to be jealous of Allie, but she could actually feel the magnetism of their attraction to each other. Jenna would kill for what Allie had.

Jenna sighed and pulled out her phone and looked at her contacts. She scrolled down to Jeff's name and then pushed delete. She went to her messages with Jeff and without reading any of them she deleted those too. Allie was wrong when she said Jeff was harmless. Jenna's broken heart was proof of that and she would make sure that no one would ever know.

Jenna stubbed out her cigarette and walked back inside. Cara and the cute guy had moved back out onto the dance floor alongside Allie and Jeff. Kym was dancing with Jamal, and Jenna began to feel resentful as she ordered another shot with a beer chaser. After the song ended Kym walked over to Jenna who had a fresh drink in her hand and was chatting with the bartender. Are you ready to go?" Kym asked. "It's almost closing time."

Cara walked up holding her jacket. Jenna took another gulp of her drink and looked over at Allie. "Allie doesn't look ready."

Kym smiled and said, "Allie said she's staying here with Jeff and he'll drop her off sometime tomorrow."

Of course. Jenna forced herself to not look Allie's way and finished her beer followed by one last shot and then said, "I'm ready."

Jenna fished around in the pocket of her jacket for her keys and pulled them out.

Chapter 13
Interrogation

Jenna was stunned into silence and stared at the police officer standing next to her hospital bed. He continued to look at her and then glanced at her mother and said, "Ma'am I'm going to have to ask you to leave the room."

Mom looked from Jenna to the doctor. "Can't this wait until she's feeling better? She's lucky to be alive and she's just had surgery."

The doctor spoke up, "I will stay with her. If this interferes with her recovery, then I will stop it."

Mom looked at the two men and then down at Jenna. She pushed Jenna's hair away from her forehead and kissed it. "I'll call Mark, our attorney. Everything will be okay Jenna. Don't say anything until he gets here," Mom said glaring at the officer as she walked towards the door.

Jenna looked at the officer her heart beating rapidly. "What happened?" He had just read Jenna her rights and still no one had told her what happened. She closed her eyes and tried to remember. *Cara's dead? I killed Cara? None of this makes sense!* She tried to compose herself. She studied the officer as he took a seat in the chair that her mom had vacated and watched as he pulled a notebook and pen out of his pocket. She was surprised to see that he wasn't much older than her. His short dark hair and piercing dark eyes showed that he expected cooperation. He looked down at Jenna and her heart sank. She was being arrested and questioned like a criminal.

"Jenna." His voice demanded respect. "I know you've been through a lot, but I'd like to ask you a few questions." He looked down at his notebook and then back at her.

Tears started spilling out of her eyes and she wasn't sure if it was her injuries or fear that was making it difficult to breathe. The doctor came over to check Jenna's vitals and looked at her. "Do you want me to make him leave?"

She shook her head no. Jenna could tell the officer was surprised.

She motioned to the glass of water that was sitting on the table next to the officer. He picked up the glass and handed it to her. She tried to reach for it, but a sharp pain shot through her arm and she winced.

He cleared his throat and said, "Here, let me help." He held the glass closer to her and guided the straw into her mouth. Better?" he asked.

Jenna nodded. She looked at him and willed her mouth to speak. "Can you tell me what happened?" she asked.

He set the glass down on the table and then looked back at her. "I was hoping you could do the same," he said sounding professional again.

“I don’t remember. You said that Cara is dead?” He nodded. Tears trailed down Jenna’s face. She couldn’t talk, she couldn’t breathe, and she started to shake uncontrollably.

The doctor came over and began checking her vitals again. He looked at the police officer. “I’m going to have to ask you to leave.”

The officer nodded and stood up. He was tall and lean. He looked at her with regret and said, “We’ll talk when you’re feeling better.”

Doctor Andrews inserted a sedative into Jenna’s IV. She watched as the liquid dripped through the line. Her mother had slipped silently back into the room unbeknownst to Jenna. She saw the lights growing dimmer and dimmer until she saw nothing at all.

It was two days later before Jenna began feeling more like herself. She no longer felt groggy and when she opened her eyes she saw her mother still sitting by her side. Sitting next to her mother was whom she presumed to be “Mark, the attorney.” He was sifting through papers and making notes from time to time. Jenna quietly studied him. He was a bit paunchy with a head full of dark curly hair and round glasses. He wore a dark suit and appeared to be in his fifties. Just by looking at him Jenna could tell that he was very self-confident. She closed her eyes and thought about Cara. She couldn’t believe that she was gone. Cara was so young, and she was doing great things with her life. Jenna was astounded that she was being blamed for Cara’s death.

She closed her eyes again trying to take herself back to that night but she was interrupted by a quick knock on the door as Dr. Andrews entered with a police officer right behind him. He glanced around the room and offered a nod when he saw Jenna's mother. Her mother straightened up and gave a curt nod as she walked stiffly out the door. Mark stayed in the room as introductions were made.

The officer looked at Jenna with his dark endless eyes and cleared his throat. "Hi, Jenna, I'm Officer Cortland. I was on the scene of the accident and I'd like to ask you a few questions if you are feeling up to it."

She looked over at Mark who nodded his head giving me permission to speak. Jenna sat up straighter in her bed and nervously smoothed down her hair. "I'll try," she replied.

Mark cleared his throat and Jenna tried to ignore him. Officer Cortland looked over at Mark. He took a seat next to Jenna's bed, and opened his notebook.

He smiled encouragingly and said, "Would you please state your name?"

Jenna looked at him and said, "Jenna Renee Lewis."

He continued writing. "What is your address?"

Jenna licked her cracked lips. "Can I have a sip of water please?"

Mark looked up from taking notes but Officer Cortland was already on his feet. "Here you go," he said gently easing the straw into her mouth.

She took a long sip and then leaned back. "Thank you, my address is 1334 West Chestnut Street."

Officer Cortland studied her intently and then asked, "Can you tell me what you were doing on the night of March 25th?"

Jenna thought about it. *What was today? She didn't even know.* Jenna cleared her throat and tried to think back to that horrendous night. "I really can't remember much," she said. Both men wrote this down in their notebooks.

"That's okay," the officer said dismissively. "Can you tell me the names of your roommates?"

Jenna smiled sadly remembering Cara. "Cara Donnelly, Kym Syndako, and Allie Stratford." Tears started dripping from her eyes as she thinks of Cara. Officer Cortland instantly handed her a tissue. "Thanks," Jenna said gratefully.

Officer Cortland continued, "Where were you on the night of March 25th?"

Jenna thinks back and replied, "Earlier that day I had gone to class and then back home. My friend Kym had just lost her father. He had a massive heart attack and she was upset."

Jenna stopped and paused to think. Her head began to ache and she adjusted her pillow so that she was lying back more.

"What happened next?" Officer Cortland asked.

"I remember talking with Kym about her dad and we were all drinking."

"Who was drinking?" asked Officer Cortland. Jenna cleared her throat, "Kym, Cara, Allie, and myself."

"Were you drinking at home or did you go out?" the officer asked.

Jenna thought for a moment and said, "I remember that all of us had walked down to Mulcahey's Pub." She hesitated. "It's difficult to remember much after that."

Officer Cortland pressed on, "Did you go anywhere else?"

Jenna thought for a while and said, "I vaguely remember something about going to Trent's house and punching him. I don't know why I would do that though..." She closed her eyes and tried to think back. "Wait, I wasn't the one driving it was Allie."

Mark and the officer both look at her in surprise. "Are you sure?" Officer Cortland asks.

"Yes," Jenna replied excitedly, "I handed the keys to Allie and she drove." She breathed a sigh of relief. This had all been a misunderstanding.

Officer Cortland looked at his notes again and said, "I think you might be mistaken. According to my notes Allie Stratford wasn't in the car at the time of the accident. She was at Mickey's Hideout." Jenna thought for a minute and began to remember watching Jeff and Allie cuddled up in a corner booth. Her breathing became shallower and her chest tightened. Her head was pounding, and she knew that she was having a panic attack. She pressed the button for a nurse who instantly entered the room with a smile on her face. The nurse looked confused when she spotted the police officer and a man in a dark suit looking back at her in surprise.

Jenna broke the silence and addressed the nurse. "I'm having a panic attack. Can I please have something for it?"

The nurse walked over to Jenna's chart and picked it up. She made a note on it and gave her a dose of medication to calm her anxiety. The medication worked quickly and soon Jenna began to feel groggy.

Mark cleared his throat and looked directly at the police officer. "My client needs to rest. As you can see she is still recovering."

Officer Cortland looked at Jenna who had already closed her eyes. He flipped his notebook shut and stuffed it in his pocket. He looked at Jenna for a minute wondering what she's hiding. He wasn't sure, but he intended to find out. He nodded silently at Mark and left the room.

When Jenna finally opened her eyes, it was dark outside. The room was empty except for the machines beeping behind her. It felt strange being alone. Her mother was usually sitting in a chair beside her. The nurse came in to take her vitals and refresh her water. She handed the glass to Jenna. "Is there anything else you need?" the young nurse asked.

Jenna tried not to cry again as she looked at the nurse thinking about how Cara will never have that chance. *How did this happen?* Jenna clears her throat and says, "Is Officer Cortland still outside my room?" The nurse nodded hesitantly not wanting to upset Jenna. "Could you ask him to come in please?"

The nurse looked up in surprise. "Are you sure?"

Jenna shook her head, "Yes, I'm sure."

The nurse finished checking all of Jenna's vitals then left the room sending in Officer Cortland. He looked surprised as he stepped through the door and glanced around the room. "You wanted to see me?" he asked.

Jenna smiled and nodded. "Would you like your lawyer present?" he asked.

Jenna hesitated for a minute before she said, "I just want to talk. Is that okay?"

He stood there not quite knowing what she wanted from him. He cleared his throat, "Sure." He pulled out his notebook and pencil.

"Wait," Jenna said. "I already told you I don't remember anything else. I don't want to talk about the accident. I just want to talk."

He tucked his notebook back into his pocket and sat down in a nearby chair. "What would you like to talk about?"

"Well, for starters what's your name?" Jenna asked.

He looked uncomfortable but answered her question, "Eric."

"How long have you been a police officer?"

"This is my third year on the force," he replied proudly.

"Well, Eric, you seem like a nice guy. Even if you are trying to arrest me for something I don't think I did."

He smiled but his eyes pierced right through her. "What makes you think that you didn't do it?"

Jenna shrugged. "Just a feeling I have. If I did kill my best friend don't you think I would remember?" She didn't wait for a reply. "Can I ask you something off the record?"

"Maybe," he replied.

"Can you tell me what happened?"

"That would be breaching protocol, so the answer is no."

"Is there anything you can tell me?" she asked. "I know it sounds stupid but every time I bring it up my mom instantly changes the subject or tells me she'll explain it all later. I haven't seen either of my friends and my dad is nonexistent. My lawyer should know the whole story but today was the first day that I've seen him and that was when you walked into the room. Please? Maybe it'll help jar my memory."

Eric looked at her for a long time then blew out a long sigh. "I guess I can tell you the details that are public knowledge. Who knows, maybe it'll help."

Jenna leaned back ready to listen.

"If it gets to be too much let me know, okay?" Eric ordered.

She smiled. "Okay."

Eric started, "At approximately three a.m. a 911 call came across the scanner. I was one of the first to arrive at the scene. A vehicle was upside down in the middle of the road. We have determined that no other vehicles were involved in the crash. Cara was pronounced dead at the scene."

Jenna's eyes started tearing up again and she looked up at the ceiling to try to prevent them from sliding down her cheeks.

"Do you want me to stop?" Eric asked gently.

Jenna gazed into his endless brown eyes. "No, keep going."

Eric shifted uncomfortably in his chair. "No one was wearing a seatbelt and you and Kym were ejected from the car."

Jenna leaned back and gasped, "Oh my god."

He looked at her quizzically, but she nodded indicating for him to keep going. "You were the last to be found. I was the one who found you. I wasn't sure you were going to make it." He smiled. "I'm glad you did."

"What happened to Allie and Kym?" Jenna asked.

Eric shrugged. "Kym Syndako was taken to a different hospital to be treated for her injuries and Allie Stratford wasn't there. Apparently, she had stayed back at Mickey's Hideout."

Jenna thought back and said, "That's right, you mentioned that earlier. Sorry, I guess I'm still a little groggy from the medications they keep pumping into me.

"Has Kym been released?" Jenna asked.

"I really don't know. I've been assigned to you."

"Why do you think it was me?"

Eric shifted uneasily in his chair. "I'm not able to tell you that."

"Sorry, I just don't remember and was hoping to understand how this happened."

Eric stood up and said, "I really should be going and I'm sure you want to rest." He walked towards the door.

"Eric?" Jenna said hesitantly. Eric turned.

"Thank you," she whispered. Eric nodded and left.

Chapter 14
The Charges

Mark walked into the room with an air of authority. He sat down and explained the charges to Jenna and went over the statement that she had given to Officer Cortland. She still had a difficult time remembering what happened although when Mark slowly walked her through her statement she began to remember small bits and pieces of that night. It was excruciating reliving it, knowing that her best friend was dead.

"What about your drug use?" Mark had asked.

"What drug use?" Jenna asked bewildered. "I wasn't using drugs. Why are they accusing me of using drugs?"

Mark looked down at his notes. "It says here that you had more than the required prescription in your system."

She looked at him trying to remember. "I don't usually take more than what's prescribed, but that day was awful. I came home and discovered that Kym's father had died. I was sitting in her room talking to her about my own father. I remember feeling a panic attack coming on, so I took a

Clonazapam, which by the way, was prescribed to me by my doctor. Later that night, we walked to the bar and things were fine. We left and drove to Trent's house. I remember after Cara flipped out over Trent and climbed behind the wheel that I freaked out and took another one."

Mark looked down at the charges again. "They also registered your alcohol consumption as .150 mg/dL. According to the doctor's notes, the medication that you were prescribed and alcohol should not be taken together which might account for your loss in memory. It's really important, Jenna, if you remember anything, anything at all, then you have to tell me. I need to know everything if I'm going to help you."

Jenna sighed and sank back farther on her pillow. "I wish I could. I know I wasn't driving, you've got to believe me." Her eyes filled with tears. "What about Kym or Allie? Can't one of them vouch for me?"

Mark looked back at his notes. "According to the police report, Kym stated that you were the driver." Mark flipped to another page and continued, "And according to the information from the police department, it is conceivable based on where you were ejected that you could have been the driver." He flipped to another page. "As far as the details about Allie, she states that she wasn't in the car at the time." Mark looked expectantly at Jenna.

Jenna looked at him quizzically. "Where was Allie? Maybe she saw who was driving?"

Mark looked at his paper. "She reported that she stayed behind in Mickey's Hideout with someone by the name of

Jeff Hamilton. The police also have a copy of the security footage from inside Mickey's Pub proving her statement. It also shows you drinking heavily, putting on your jacket, and then holding your keys in your hand when you left. The security camera stationed in the parking lot was broken so there is only circumstantial evidence that you were the driver."

Jenna closed her eyes trying to remember. She remembered Cara talking and dancing with some guy at the bar. She remembered talking to Kym. She remembered Cara and Kym asking her if she was ready to go. She faintly remembered Allie curled up with Jeff in a booth. She remembered walking outside and lighting a cigarette and feeling heartsick by seeing how awestruck Jeff was with Allie. She had gone to the car and pulled out another Clonazapam to drown out her misery.

Jenna opened her eyes in surprise and looked at Mark. "I did take more than I was prescribed." She leaned forward earnestly, "I didn't do it on purpose. It was an honest mistake." Jenna explained how her last pill came about. Mark took notes as Jenna gave him this new information.

Jenna asked, "Mark?"

"Yes?"

"Based on the information you have what do you think my chances are?"

Mark cleared his throat and looked up at her adjusting his glasses. "It's hard to say. I never know how a jury will decide. The prosecutor has to prove their case beyond a reasonable doubt. As long as we can infuse a sense of doubt in the case then you may be able to have your sentence lessened or dismissed altogether." He leaned forward and said seriously, "I'm not going to sugarcoat this for you Jenna, even though the evidence is circumstantial, the state has a strong case. That's why it's so important that you tell me everything you remember."

Jenna blinked back tears. "I'm trying. I'm *really* trying."

Mark replied patiently, "I know." He stood up and walked towards the door. "I'll let you get some rest."

Mark opened the door to leave. "Mark?" Jenna asked.

He turned to look. "Yes."

"What happens next?"

Mark looked at Jenna and said, "Once you are released from the hospital then you'll be taken into custody. There will be a hearing and you will enter a plea of not guilty."

Jenna still couldn't believe this was happening. She couldn't even speak, she nodded in understanding. Mark mumbled good night and left quietly.

Jenna picked up the remote and aimlessly flipped through the channels trying to find something to distract her. There was a knock on the door and Dr. Andrew's walked in holding her chart. "Hello, Jenna," he said cheerily. "How are you feeling today?"

Jenna forced herself to smile. "Each day I feel a little better."

He looked her chart over and took her vitals. "Your vitals look stable and your leg is healing nicely. I see no reason to keep you here any longer. Congratulations, you will be released in the morning."

Jenna looked at him panic stricken. She couldn't speak so she nodded as he looked at her sympathetically, gently squeezed her hand, and walked towards the door.

"Dr. Andrews?"

"Yes, Jenna?"

"Has Officer Cortland arrived yet?"

Dr. Andrew's looked at her sadly. "He got here about ten minutes ago."

Jenna asked, "Could you send him in please?"

He nodded yes and quietly stepped out of the room.

Jenna sat back stunned at the doctor's news. She heard a sudden burst of laughter and noticed that she was still holding the remote in her hand. She looked up to see that her channel surfing has landed on 'Friends'. Everyone looked so happy and carefree. Kind of how her life had been before the accident, before Kym's father died, before Cara decided to find out what Trent had been hiding for god knew how long.

There was a knock on the door and Officer Cortland poked his head in the doorway. "You wanted to see me?"

Jenna nodded yes and turned off the television.

He walked in and sat in the chair beside her bed. It was quiet for a few minutes and then he asked, "How are you feeling?"

Jenna smiled sadly. "Better. In fact, I'm being released tomorrow."

"I know," he said quickly, then instantly regretted his quick reply. "Sorry."

Jenna rolled her eyes and tried to blink back the tears. *Of course, he would know already.*

"What's going to happen to me?" she asked.

He looked at her confused. "What do you mean?"

Jenna looked at him earnestly. "What is going to happen to me tomorrow?

He cleared his throat and said, "Well, first you will be released into our custody where we will take you to the station. Then, you will be fingerprinted and detained until your first initial hearing."

The room was silent again as Eric sat there uncomfortably. He had gotten a soft spot for Jenna, a trait that could prove deadly in his profession, but he was beginning to believe that this was just a case of drinking too much and driving. It wasn't like she had intentionally set out to hurt anyone. It was sad, and he knew she would live with many regrets for the rest of her life.

Jenna finally said, "Can I ask you something Eric?"

He cleared his throat. "Sure."

"Will you be the one taking me into custody?"

He shook his head. "No, I'm the night shift. I'm not sure what time they are releasing you but I'm sure I won't be in yet.

"Oh," she said, resting her head back and sighing heavily.

"Why do you ask?"

She laughed bitterly. "I know this is crazy and I'm the bad guy here, so I deserve this, but I trust you. I'm scared."

Eric tried not to look surprised. "If it would make you feel better I could probably show up and oversee things. I wouldn't be the arresting officer, but I would at least be someone you know when you are being processed."

Jenna smiled sadly. "I'm sorry. I shouldn't be burdening you with my problems. You don't have to come."

Eric nodded in agreement but was torn between wanting to help this girl who was beginning to grow on him and maintaining a professional relationship.

Eric replied, "You'll be fine. We are not bad people."

Jenna took a deep breath and couldn't look at him. "No, you're not. I am."

There was a knock on the door and Jenna's mother walked in carrying a small suitcase. "Am I interrupting something?"

Eric jumped up and said, "No, I think we're done here." He hastily made his way to the door before he said something he'd regret like *It was just an accident. You're a good person.* He couldn't risk getting emotionally involved.

Chapter 15
Booking

The next morning a young nurse entered Jenna's room with a handful of discharge papers. She went through and explained what each paper said and Jenna dutifully signed them. Jenna's mind wasn't on her discharge but instead on her upcoming incarceration. She still couldn't believe that this was really happening. Once everything had been signed, the nurse gathered up the paperwork and exited the room.

Soon after, a police officer who identified himself as Officer Modesko, entered the room with his partner, Officer Lambert. Officer Modesko walked up to Jenna and said, "Are you ready Jenna?"

She wiped a tear from her face, took in a deep shaky breath, and nodded. The nurse came in pushing a wheelchair. Jenna stood up and used her crutches to help her move from the bed to the wheelchair. The nurse pushed Jenna through the hallway of the hospital while the two police officers followed beside her. People gawked at her as she was being wheeled out. Jenna had always hated attention, but this brought her to an all new level of low.

Jenna had to shield her eyes from the glaring sun once they had reached the outside of the hospital. It was a warm, sunny day. The sky was bright blue with white billowing clouds floating overhead. On any other day like this Jenna would have been wearing her bathing suit and lying on the beach. She didn't foresee any days like that for a very long time.

The police car was already parked in front of the hospital. She stood up using her crutches. She turned and thanked the nurse and then maneuvered herself towards the police car. The two men flanked each side of her. Jenna rolled her eyes and said angrily, "I'm on crutches do you really think I will try and make a run for it?" Neither man said a word as one of them opened the back door for her to get inside and the other walked over to the driver's seat. Once she was seated in the car the officer pulled out a pair of handcuffs and clasped them tightly on Jenna's wrists. Once again, she rolled her eyes, but this time didn't say a word. She could see people walking past staring openly at her while other people standing outside pretended to be nonchalant while sneaking peeks her way. Jenna shrunk down in her seat and wished she could just disappear.

The car started rolling slowly forward and Jenna felt beads of sweat gathering on her forehead as she tried to imagine what jail was going to be like. She had never been in an actual jail but had watched plenty of them on reality television. She tried to turn her brain off by looking out the window. It was one of those perfect days that wasn't too hot or too cool. The type of day that beckons you to be outside going shopping with your friends or driving down to the lake, not going to jail.

They rode in silence to the police station. Jenna continued looking out the window as buildings and people whirred past her. She wondered what they were doing, where they were going, how they chose to spend the normalcy of their life. She closed her eyes and focused on her breathing to try to ward off a panic attack. The police officers had immediately taken her medication and she knew she would have to wait to see a medical officer before they would allow her to take anything and then only with someone watching her.

The car pulled up to the police station and parked. Officer Modesko opened Jenna's door and extracted her crutches from the car. He held them for her as she climbed out and balanced a crutch on each side. She slowly made her way into the station. She walked into the dimly lit building pausing to allow her eyes to re-adjust so that she could see. She was directed to a chair in front of Officer Modesko's desk and he pulled up her file. He focused on his computer screen and said, "Can you please verify your name?"

She cleared her throat. "Jenna Renee Lewis."

"Who is your person of contact?" he asked without looking up.

"Why would you need to know that?" Jenna asked.

The officer looked over at her. "In case something happens... uh... while you're incarcerated." Her heart sank even further, and she tried to take a deep breath to push down the panic.

Jenna thought for a moment. Her friends have deserted her, her father couldn't stand to look at her, and although her mother bursts into tears every time they were in the same room at least she was there. She answered, "My mother, Leanne Lewis."

Officer Modesko continued typing. "It appears you have a prescription for Clonazapam and Lithium is that correct?"

"Yes, sir," replied Jenna.

Officer Modesko continued typing and then finally sat back in his chair. The light on his phone was continuously blinking but if he noticed he didn't do anything about it. He stood up and said, "Come with me."

Jenna wasn't sure where she was going but did it matter? She knew where she was going to end up. She looked around hoping to catch a glance of Eric, but she didn't see him. Her heart sank but it wasn't his fault. She was a convict, a nobody, someone he could care less about. Jenna hobbled after the officer as he led her into a sterile white room and ordered her to stand against the wall. She started to shake but did as he asked. "Look into the camera," he ordered.

Jenna raised her eyes from the floor to the camera and saw Eric standing next to him. He smiled sadly and nodded his head. She took a deep breath, trying to calm her nerves, and looked into the camera. Officer Modesko then said, "Turn to the side." She did, and he clicked a picture of her profile.

Eric didn't say a word as the officer escorted Jenna to another room where she was fingerprinted. She felt better knowing that Eric was there. His silent presence made her feel as though maybe someone cared. She continued following directions as the officer led here to another room where she was searched and given an orange jumpsuit to wear. Jenna hung her head in shame as she was escorted back to the holding cell. She sat in silence, leaning her head back against the bars, looking at the ceiling. She had never felt so alone. Jenna would give anything to have her old life back. How could she have been driving? How could she have been so stupid? If it weren't for her Cara would still be alive. She deserves everything that happens to her. She angrily brushed away a tear.

Jenna heard a door click open and turned her head. Eric walked in and smiled sadly. She tried to smile back but failed miserably. "Your lawyer is here," he said.

She looked past Eric to see Mark standing in a dark suit and red tie. He was holding a briefcase and was waiting for her to be escorted to another room where they would meet to discuss her case. Jenna slowly stood up, her heart beating in her chest. She took a deep breath and reminded herself that she deserved this. She would accept the consequences of her actions.

Mark wasn't smiling when they walked into the room. Jenna hobbled over to a chair and sat down. Her hands were shaking so she placed them in her lap trying to keep them still. Mark pulled out a stack of papers and stated formally, "In a few minutes you are going to be escorted into the courtroom. You will stand before the judge and he will read the charges against you. The judge will ask you how do you plead, and you will respond with not guilty."

Jenna interrupted him, "What if I am guilty?"

He looked up in surprise. "Is there a new development that I should know about?"

Jenna leaned back in her chair and looked at the ceiling. "If the evidence points to me being the cause of Cara's death then I deserve whatever is coming to me. I will accept the consequences."

Mark leaned towards Jenna and said in a controlled voice, "The evidence is circumstantial. You will plead not guilty, do you understand?" It wasn't a question but more like an order.

Jenna nodded silently and listened as Mark continued talking as though the conversation had never happened. "The judge will give further instructions as to when your next hearing will be and what the conditions of your bail will be. Do you understand?"

No! I want to shout. I don't understand how any of this can be happening. NO! I don't understand! Instead Jenna shook her head and felt like someone who just witnessed something horrific and was in shock.

Chapter 16
Not Guilty

Jenna followed Mark into the courtroom and stood beside him balancing herself on her crutches. The room was intimidating, and Jenna began to feel dizzy. She was certain she was going to be sick. She started to sit but Mark motioned for her to stand. The judge looked down at Jenna's file and read the charges to himself, then he cleared his throat and announced in a loud clear voice. "Jenna Renee Lewis, you have been charged with one count of operating a vehicle under the influence of drugs, one count of driving while intoxicated, and one count of vehicular homicide in the death of Cara Jenkins."

Jenna placed her hands on the table to help her continue standing as things started going black. The judge looked over his glasses and asked, "How do you plead?"

Jenna opened her mouth to speak but nothing came out. She was having difficulty breathing.

Mark looked at her and instructed her to take a deep breath. She did so and then he nodded to encourage her to answer the judge. She tried again and this time she found her voice. "Not guilty."

The judge then replied, "Based on the defendant's cooperation with the police department and the court recognizes that she is still recovering from an accident, the defendant will be released on $10,000 bail. Jenna, you will also be required to refrain from drugs or alcohol. You must remain within the state and have no contact with any of the witnesses. Do you understand these conditions, Miss Lewis?"

Jenna nodded and replied, "Yes, Your Honor."

Mark looked at the judge and said, "Thank you, Your Honor." He turned towards Jenna and led her out of the courtroom.

Jenna sat in her cell wondering what would happen now. A few hours later Mark walked in escorted by a police officer. "Your mother is working on the paperwork right now. With any luck you'll be free to go home soon."

Home, that word seemed so foreign to her now.

The next day Jenna was released into her mother's custody. She had never been so relieved to be away from a place in her life. She hobbled through a hallway escorted by Officer Modesko and saw that her mother was waiting for her in the waiting area. Her face lit up when she saw her daughter. Jenna hobbled over and she hugged her mom tightly as they both openly cried. Jenna collected her belongings and then followed her mother out the door. It felt so freeing to be outside with the blinding sun shining down on her. It felt like she had entered an entirely different world.

Mark had the car parked out front and tried to swiftly lead them to the car. She heard someone shouting at her and calling her a murderer as reporters began swarming to get a statement. Mark tried to hurry her along before the reporters reached them which was a difficult feat on crutches. Mark quickly opened the car door and Jenna maneuvered herself in as quickly as possible.

"Let's go," Mark ordered the driver as the reporters began to get closer. Jenna leaned her head back on the seat and closed her eyes thinking about Cara. The last time she was in a car they were together. Cara should still be alive, not her. Cara should be the one going to classes and laughing with her friends. Jenna didn't deserve to be here. She didn't know why she let Mark bully her into pleading not guilty but somewhere in the back of her mind it was still hard to believe that she did this. As hard as she tried she still couldn't remember what happened. If she did something so awful wouldn't she remember it or at least parts of it?

The ride home was quiet. Jenna hadn't seen her dad since before the accident. She still hadn't forgiven him for giving her the ultimatum of moving out or going to college. She cringed at the thought of facing him after he told her she'd have to clean up her own messes. Once again her parents were involved in her own bad decision and she would have gladly faced the guillotine instead of her father. The car stopped in front of the house. The pale yellow paint had started peeling off around the front door and the bushes in front still needed to be trimmed back. Since this nightmare started it seemed as though the world had stood still.

Mark turned off the car and Jenna opened her door. Her hands were shaking as she stood up and adjusted her crutches. She felt about a hundred years old. She noticed that Dad didn't come to greet her, and a feeling of trepidation descended upon her. This wasn't a good sign. She had always been a disappointment to her father and this is just another confirmation that she hadn't changed.

She hobbled cautiously into the living room. The drapes had been closed and it was dark except for a dimly lit lamp sitting on the small table next to her father. He was reading the paper and he looked older than the last time she had seen him. "Hi, Dad," Jenna said hesitantly. He didn't respond, and she wondered if he had heard her. She cleared her throat and sat down on the edge of the couch. "How have you been?" Jenna asked not knowing what else to say.

Dad calmly folded the paper and placed it on his lap. He looked at her. "How have I been?" he asked incredulously. He leaned back on the sofa and said, "Let's see, my daughter has been arrested for vehicular manslaughter while driving under the influence of drugs and alcohol, according to the paper, and you sit there and ask me how I am? How do you think I am Jenna?"

His voice was starting to rise and Jenna's eyes began to well with tears. "I'm sorry," she whispered.

Dad looked at her and said, "Sorry for what? What exactly are you sorry for Jenna?"

Mom came in carrying mugs of coffee. She handed one to Jenna and kept the other. She sat down next to Jenna and said in a calm voice, "Charles, it's been a long day. We're all tired and stressed. Can't we just for one night put this aside and just be thankful that Jenna's home?"

Dad looked from Mom to Jenna. He was quiet for a moment and then said, "Of course, dear, I wouldn't want to upset Jenna." He stood up and looked at Jenna. "It's not her fault that she was drinking, taking drugs, and driving. It wasn't her fault that she killed someone. It wasn't her fault that people stare at us when they walk past our house. The only house we've lived in and worked so hard to make a home that has now become collateral for her bail! Let's not upset Jenna." He walked over to the closet and took out his coat. He slipped it on.

"Charles, where are you going?" Mom asked bewildered.

"Out!" He opened the door, stomped out, and slammed the door. They could hear the squeal of the car tires as Dad drove away.

Jenna looked at her mom who was walking towards her. She pulled Jenna into her and stroked Jenna's hair as Jenna cried. Her mother's soft voice was soothing, "It's going to be okay, Jenna. Your father is worried about you. He just has a hard time showing it. It'll all work out, you'll see."

She cried and cried until there were no more tears left. Jenna pulled away and wiped her face. She looked at her mom and saw that she had been crying too. Jenna hugged her tightly and walked wearily up to her room.

She lay in her bed replaying her dad's words. *What exactly are you sorry for?* Jenna was sorry for Cara, her best friend, who didn't deserve to die. She was sorry for alienating her friends and causing them harm. She was sorry for stressing her parents out over her stupid decisions. She was sorry for herself because she was so stupid to have been driving. She could feel herself getting angry. She sat up in bed and knew that she wouldn't fall asleep. *What exactly am I sorry for?* Jenna was sorry for her whole waste of a life. At least Cara helped others, she on the other hand, was just wasted space.

Chapter 17
The Next Day

Jenna woke up to the sound of rain splattering against her window. The sound of thunder roared ominously overhead. She lay in bed thinking about how the storm seemed to reflect her life. She could hear her mom puttering downstairs and the aroma of fresh coffee lingered through the house. She could hear her father's voice as he was talking to her mom and Jenna immediately felt her stomach clench at the thought of having to face her father. She threw the blanket over her head and tried to go back to sleep but it was no use. She'd have to face him sooner or later.

Jenna climbed out of bed and slowly got dressed. She limped carefully down the stairs into the kitchen. Her dad was sitting at the table eating breakfast while her mom was doing the dishes. Mom turned around when she heard her enter the kitchen and Jenna saw that she had been crying. Dad was silent when she walked in. She opened the cupboard and took out a mug. She filled her mug with coffee and then sat at the table.

Dad stopped eating and pushed his plate away. He wiped his mouth on a napkin and looked at Jenna. "I'm sorry," he said. "I know I didn't handle things well last night."

Jenna looked at him unsure of what to say. She cleared her throat and said, "I'm sorry too, for everything. I never meant for any of this to happen." Jenna's eyes started filling up with tears. She felt like she was constantly crying and she hated it.

Mom came over and pulled out a chair beside her and sat down. Dad looked back at her and said, "I know you didn't mean for this to happen. I'm mostly upset that you made the decision to get behind the wheel after you've been drinking and that you also had drugs in your system. This combination resulted in someone's death."

Jenna hated that her dad said she was using drugs. It was a prescription for crying out loud.

Mom cleared her throat and said, "Maybe it would be helpful if Jenna explained what happened instead of us making assumptions."

Dad looked over at Mom. "Leanne, you can't deny the evidence."

Jenna interrupted, "You're right, Dad. I did have drugs in my system, but I'd like to explain. It won't change anything but maybe you might have a different opinion of me."

Dad looked at Jenna and gestured for her to explain.

"I've always felt as though I was an outsider looking in on my life. Some days I'd be high on life and other days I couldn't find the energy to climb out of bed and go to class.

Cara talked to me about her concerns and encouraged me to see a doctor. I was diagnosed with a bi-polar disorder and was given medication to stabilize my mood swings and panic attacks, and it was working. I felt like a completely new person. I was going to all my classes and bringing my grades back up."

Her mom interrupted, "So the drug that the prosecutor is referring to is a prescribed medication and not just something you took without a prescription?"

Jenna nodded. "Yes, I have the medical records to prove it."

Dad asked, "Are you able to drive while taking this medication?"

"Yes."

"Then they can't use that against you," her dad replied. "I don't understand why the prosecutor is pursuing this then."

Jenna took a deep breath and said, "There's more." She explained that Kym's father had passed away and Kym wasn't allowed to fly home. She explained how Cara had discovered that Trent was cheating on her and how she had gone crazy. She talked about Allie and Jeff and how she felt jealous. She talked about taking the Clonazapam to help her manage the anxiety of the chaos around her. She then confessed that she had taken more than she was prescribed.

She looked at her parents as they processed what she had said. "I swear I didn't know I had taken more than I was supposed to at the time."

Her dad chimed in, "Plus you were mixing it with alcohol which I'm assuming you are not supposed to be doing as well, correct?"

Jenna looked down at her hands folded on the table. "You're right. I wasn't supposed to be drinking."

Her mom asked, "Do you remember getting behind the wheel of the car? Did you realize that you were driving impaired?"

"That's just it, Mom. I remember everything from that night except for that part. I know the police said that I was the one driving but I don't remember."

"Mark has a written statement from a witness at the scene that said you were the driver," her dad explained.

"I know," Jenna replied. "But don't you think I'd remember? How could I remember everything else except for driving?"

Her dad thought for a minute. "Who else could have been driving?"

"Cara or Kym," Jenna replied. "Allie stayed at Mickey's Hideout with Jeff that night."

"Well, they obviously can't question Cara, but what about Kym? Have they questioned her?" her dad asked.

Jenna sighed. "I think so. I haven't talked to Kym since the accident."

"Maybe Mark will know," her mom suggested hopefully.

Jenna stood up and placed her coffee mug in the sink. "Maybe he will. I'm supposed to meet with him at 2:00." She looked over at her parents. “I am sorry. I know I’ve disappointed you again.”

“Honey, you didn’t disappoint us,” her mom said. “We want to help you. We’re in this together.”

Her dad came over and gave her a hug. “We’ll get through this.”

Jenna felt a huge weight being lifted from her shoulders. She hugged him back and then said, “I’d like to go for a short walk if that’s okay. Since my surgery my muscles get sore if I sit still for too long.”

“Sure, honey. Would you like company?” her mother asked.

Jenna smiled. “No thanks, Mom. I just need a little time to sort out my thoughts.”

Jenna slipped on her shoes and grabbed a light jacket. She stepped outside and was grateful that the skies had cleared out and the sun was starting to peek through the trees. She started limping down the sidewalk, taking her time, and trying to sort through the change in her dad. She was lost in thought and didn’t realize that a car had slowed down next to her until it had come to almost a complete stop. She looked over and saw that it was a police car. Her heart stopped. The passenger window rolled down and she peeked inside the car. It was Officer Copeland smiling at her.

“Hi Jenna, you’re looking much better. How are you doing?”

Jenna smiled at him. “I’m taking it day by day. I still can’t remember the accident. She paused and then said, “I know you hear this all the time, but I just have a feeling that

I didn't climb behind the wheel. I just wish I knew what happened, you know?"

Eric nodded sympathetically. "I know. Head trauma is a difficult thing."

Jenna looked over the top of his car towards the park across the street. "I know you can't be fraternizing with the criminal, but I can't talk to any of my friends and I could really use a friend right now."

Eric thought for a minute and then said, "Sure, can you give me about half an hour? I'm just getting off work and I'll run home and change. Would you like to grab a cup of coffee at the Java Cafe?"

Jenna smiled. "I'd like that. I'll meet you there."

Eric smiled and put his patrol car in drive and slowly rolled away. She strolled over to the park and sat on a bench facing the lake. There were two ducks floating on top of the water with baby ducks trailing behind. She watched as two little girls squealed in delight at the edge of the lake throwing bread crumbs to the ducks and watching in fascination as the ducks started swimming toward them. She smiled, *Life used to be so simple.*

She looked at her watch and stood up from the bench. She started walking toward the Java Cafe. Quaint little shops were opening for the day and people were animated as they were laughing and talking as she walked by. She stepped into the cafe and smelled the fragrant aroma of coffee. She looked around and saw Eric sitting at a small round table towards the back of the room sipping out of a tall cup and in the center of the table were two enormous muffins sitting on a small plate. Jenna walked up to the counter and placed her order for coffee. She pulled out her wallet to pay, "No charge," replied the barista. "It's already been taken care of." She followed the cashier's eyes towards Eric and smiled. Jenna thanked the young girl and walked to their table.

She pulled out a chair and sat down. "Thanks for the coffee," Jenna said gratefully.

Eric smiled. "You're welcome."

She took a sip and rolled her eyes. "This is so good." She sat back and looked at him. She took in his short dark hair, his brown eyes, and his muscular figure. He was wearing blue jeans and a white T-shirt that stretched over his broad chest. She couldn't help but notice his tan muscular arms and she suddenly felt self-conscious.

He took a sip of coffee and put down his cup. "So, Jenna, tell me something about yourself besides the fact that you are taking life day by day."

She took another sip and asked, "What would you like to know?"

He thought for a minute and then said, "What were you majoring in college?"

Jenna laughed and said, "Law. Seems a bit ironic now don't you think?"

He smiled and said, "I don't know. I think you'd make a great lawyer. I wouldn't give up on the idea."

Jenna quit smiling and then asked, "Do you think I did it?"

Eric looked at her solemnly and said, "I don't know. It's possible."

Jenna turned her head and looked out the window then she turned back to Eric. "You know what bothers me the most?" she asked earnestly and didn't wait for him to reply. "It's the not knowing. I just can't believe I was that stupid."

Eric shifted uncomfortably. "I really can't discuss an ongoing case with you."

Jenna looked at him and smiled ruefully. "Especially when it involves me."

He shrugged and then leaned forward. "Can I suggest something?"

"Sure," she said.

"Have you ever thought about hypnosis?" he asked.

"Hypnosis? As in when I snap my finger you will act like a chicken, hypnosis?" she repeated skeptically. "I don't believe in that stuff."

Eric shrugged and said, "There have been numerous scientific studies which showed that hypnosis has been known to help people who have endured a traumatic encounter. It might help you fill in some of the holes."

Jenna smiled, "Right about now I am willing to try just about anything. Thanks, I'll look into it."

They were quiet for a moment until she asked, "Why did you decide to become a cop?"

He smiled and took a muffin from the middle of the table. He motioned to Jenna to take the other one. "My grandfather was a cop, my father was a cop, so naturally I became a cop."

"I bet your father and grandfather are quite proud," Jenna said.

"Well, my grandfather is but my father was killed in the line of duty when I was five."

"Oh wow! I'm really sorry," Jenna replied touching his hand.

She looked down startled and yanked back her hand. Eric shrugged. "Thanks, and yes he would probably be proud. He was a great man and my mom made sure I knew him even though he wasn't around."

"If your dad was killed in the line of duty why would you want to pursue such a dangerous career knowing what could happen to you?"

Eric swallowed another bite of muffin and said, "That's easy. I like helping people. What happened to my dad was a terrible thing, but he was the same way. He sacrificed his life helping a family. He was called to a domestic dispute. A husband was abusing his wife and kids. One of the boys called 911 and when my dad arrived the father was going after one of the boys and beating him pretty bad. My dad tried to stop it, but the guy had a gun hidden in the drawer next to him. He grabbed it. There was a standoff. Both shots went off at the same time. My dad killed the abusive man but later my dad passed away during surgery."

Jenna looked at him and said, "Wow that's quite a story. I'm not so sure I could have followed in his footsteps."

Eric looked serious and said earnestly, "Because of my dad that kid had a chance. His family had a chance. The kid who was beaten is now my partner and best friend. We both know the sacrifice but to us it's worth it. We try every day to make the world a better place."

"Well, I am very glad you were able to help me! If it weren't for you I might not be here either. So, thank you." Jenna said gratefully.

Eric smiled. "You're welcome."

"It sounds like you and your partner are a lot alike," Jenna said taking a sip of coffee.

Eric laughed. "In many ways we are the exact opposites. He's a family man. I'm single. He sees the lighter side of things and I'm more serious. He also tells a great joke. Me? I mess up the punchline."

Jenna laughed. "I'd like to meet him someday."

Jenna looked down at her watch and frowned. "I hate to say this, but I have to go. I have a meeting with Mark in an hour?"

"Is Mark your boyfriend?" Eric asked starting to get up.

Jenna laughed, "I have enough on my plate at the moment. I don't think there will be a boyfriend in my future for a very long time. Mark is my lawyer."

Jenna couldn't tell for sure, but she thought she saw a brief look of relief cross Eric's face. He walked her to the door and looked down at her. "Do you want a ride home?"

Jenna looked up at the bright blue sky and for the first time in a long time she almost felt normal. "No thanks," she replied. "I'll walk."

His eyes twinkled as he looked down at her. "Well, take care of yourself, Jenna."

He pulled out his keys. Jenna looked up at him and smiled. "You too, Eric. Stay safe." She turned and started walking home.

Chapter 18
Mark

Jenna stepped inside the house and was surprised to see Mark already sitting at the table talking to her parents. "Am I late?" Jenna asked panicked.

"No, not at all," Mark replied. "Your dad asked me to come a little early to catch him up on the case. I was just explaining to him that it's confidential without your permission."

Jenna looked at her father in surprise.

"I thought you'd be home earlier." He confessed. "I wasn't trying to overstep my bounds, Jenna, I was just trying to be supportive."

Jenna was astounded. *Is this the same man who is the first to believe the worst in me?* She smiled at her dad and said, "Of course it's all right. I apologize for being so late. I ran into a friend and we had coffee together. Time went by faster than I realized."

Jenna sat next to Mark as he went over his notes and the evidence against her. When he was finished Jenna asked, "I can't believe that I've never asked this but how is Kym?"

Mark looked back down at his notes and said, "She's fine. She sustained some minor injuries but nothing life threatening. She was lucky considering no one was wearing a seatbelt.

Her dad looked gravely at Jenna. "According to the reports you weren't wearing a seatbelt. You were very lucky."

Jenna took a shaky breath. "I know. I can't believe I was so stupid."

Mark cleared his throat. "You cannot have any contact with Kym or Allie, do you understand?" Jenna nodded.

Mark shuffled some papers and then took out a sheet with the outline of a car on it. "Can you label where everyone was sitting when you left Mickey's Hideout?"

Jenna picked up the pencil and her hand started to shake as she drew Cara sitting in the passenger seat. She moved her hand over to the driver's seat, but she couldn't bring herself to do it. She couldn't draw herself there. It didn't feel right."

"Is something wrong?" Mark asked.

Jenna looked up at him, "I can't do it. I don't remember." She put the pencil down still shaking.

"It's okay," Mark replied. "We'll try again later." He looked back down at his notebook. "The trial has been scheduled for August seventeenth at eight a.m. We have a lot to do between now and then."

Jenna sat quietly thinking and then said, “My friend, the one I had coffee with, suggested that sometimes hypnosis can help jar a person’s memory if they’ve had a traumatic experience. Do you think that would help? I’d be willing to try it.”

Mark took off his glasses. “Hypnosis is usually not admissible in a court of law because there are other factors that can change the outcome but at this point Jenna anything will help. Make an appointment and let me know if you remember anything. It could be a starting point to investigate.”

Jenna went to her room and pulled up the phone number for the police department on her laptop. She quickly dialed the number before she changed her mind. “May I speak with Officer Copeland?” she asked.

“Just a minute and I’ll transfer you,” the receptionist replied.

Jenna waited nervously and was immediately transferred to Eric’s voicemail. “Hi Eric, this is Jenna. I have decided to take your advice and was wondering if you could recommend someone who practices hypnosis?” She hung up. Of course, he wouldn’t be there. He had just gotten off of work. Ten minutes later Jenna’s phone rang. “Hello?”

“Hi, Jenna, I just got your message. I would recommend you try Dr. Carlyle. She’s had terrific results with patients.”

“Okay, thanks. I’ll give her a try.”

There was an awkward silence, so she said, “Well, I’ve got to go. Thank you again for today.”

“You’re welcome,” Eric replied.

Jenna looked up Dr. Carlyle’s number, dialed, and made an appointment for the next day.

Chapter 19
Hypnosis

The next day Jenna pulled into the parking lot of Dr. Carlyle's office. It was part of the Bailey Medical Center. The building was bustling when Jenna walked in. People were registering for appointments, nurses were calling patient's names, and somewhere in the corner a baby was crying. Jenna walked up to the information desk and asked for directions to Dr. Carlyle's office. Her mother had offered to come with her, but she was nervous as it was and insisted she go alone.

Dr. Carlyle's office was down a long barren hallway. The floors looked freshly waxed and the smell of antiseptic was prevalent. Once she reached the end of the hallway she walked through a door and everything looked dramatically different. A patterned carpet in soothing colors covered the floor. There were pictures of mountainous landscapes hanging on the walls. Soft music was coming from the speakers overhead. A soothing water fountain was trickling in the corner. Jenna immediately felt her jitters quiet a little.

She checked in and picked up a magazine while she waited to be called. It wasn't long before she heard the receptionist's voice. "Jenna, you can go in now." Jenna nervously put down the magazine and stood up. She ran a hand through her hair, a nervous habit of hers, and walked towards the dark oak doors.

Dr. Carlyle was sitting behind a desk looking through a folder in front of her. She pushed her chair back and walked over to Jenna. She smiled easily and held out her hand. "Hi Jenna, I'm Dr. Carlyle. It's nice to meet you."

Jenna shook her hand and immediately began to feel more at ease. Dr. Carlyle wasn't how she had pictured her at all. She was tall and graceful and seemed genuinely at ease. Her dark hair was swept up in a messy bun. She wore beige linen pants, and a soft blue flowing shirt that complimented her complexion. She had twinkling blue eyes and creases near her eyes that revealed that she smiled a lot.

"Come in and have a seat while we get to know each other." Jenna sat down on a brown leather chair feeling the cushions conform to her body making her feel safe like she was surrounded in a cocoon and nothing could hurt her. On a table in front of Jenna sat a tray full of coffee, tea, cookies, and muffins.

"Would you prefer coffee or tea?" Dr. Carlyle asked expectantly.

"Coffee," Jenna replied.

Dr. Carlyle smiled. "I'm a coffee drinker too. I can't start my day without it."

Jenna laughed because she felt the same way. Dr. Carlyle handed Jenna a cup and added some cream and sugar to it. Jenna took a sip and it tasted heavenly. She offered Jenna a muffin which at first she declined but they looked so scrumptious that she couldn't help herself. She took a bite and rolled her eyes because they were as good as they looked. They talked about Jenna's family, her friends, her classes, but Dr. Carlyle did it in such a way that Jenna didn't feel like she was being interrogated. They talked about Cara and how she suggested that Jenna see a doctor which led to her being diagnosed with a bi-polar disorder. They talked about Jenna's medications and how she felt when she was taking them.

She thought of Cara and her eyes began to well up with tears. Dr. Carlyle handed Jenna a tissue and gave her time to gather her thoughts. Jenna explained to Dr. Carlyle that Cara was her best friend and that she had helped Jenna find herself more than anyone else. When Jenna had started college she was resentful and had lived up to her parents' low expectations. Jenna had really been struggling, and Cara was the one who helped her to stand on her own two feet. Once she found out she had a bi-polar disorder her mood swings made more sense. She began to feel normal and truly enjoyed being with people and doing things with her friends.

"I can see that your friends mean a lot to you," Dr. Carlyle commented. "I'm sure you mean a lot to them too."

Jenna smiled sadly. "I hope so. I miss them." Once again Cara popped into her mind.

Dr. Carlyle sat back in her chair and said, "Why don't we begin."

"Okay," Jenna replied hesitantly.

Dr. Carlyle pulled a remote from the side pocket of the chair and handed it to her. "Why don't you go ahead and get comfortable and I'll explain how the process works."

Jenna took the remote from Dr. Carlyle's hand and adjusted the chair so that she was lying back comfortably. "Hypnotherapy can help you recall things from your past. It may work or may not work it depends on how accepting you are towards hypnosis. You may experience a sense of heightened awareness and that's perfectly normal. Do you have any questions before we begin?"

Jenna adjusted herself in the chair and said, "No. I'm ready."

The therapist began. "Think of a place where you feel safe and happy. It could be a beach, the forest, your room, anywhere."

Jenna closed her eyes and envisioned the beach. She could see the gentle rolling waves, smell the salty air, feel the warm breeze washing over her and she felt so relaxed. Dr. Carlyle continued, "From your safe place I want you to think back to the day you were with Allie and Kym and Cara. You just woke up to start your day."

The room was quiet as Jenna let her thoughts start to drift back to that fateful day then Dr. Carlyle begins to speak. "What do you see?"

Jenna began in a soft voice. "It's Friday and I'm lying in bed trying to convince myself to get up for my Intro to Law class. I can hear Cara and Allie laughing and I smell coffee percolating." Jenna continues to recall every event, every sound, every feeling about that day.

Dr. Carlyle continues talking softly and an hour has gone by before Jenna begins to whimper and Dr. Carlyle interjects, "Jenna hold up one finger if you need to stop and two fingers if you're okay to continue."

Jenna holds up two fingers as she relives the moment she found out about Kym's father dying, walking down to the pub, driving to Trent's house. She talks about Cara being upset and Allie huddled up with Jeff in a booth at Mickey's Hideout. She talks about going outside to get some air and taking an extra Clonazepam. She remembers walking back into the pub and seeing Cara dancing with some guy and Kym walking towards her. Cara and Kym are ready to leave but Allie decided to stay and was out on the dance floor dancing with Jeff. Jenna shrugged and pretended that it didn't bother her as they started to walk outside. Jenna recalled pulling her keys out of her pocket as the three girls walk out the door. They were weaving their way towards the car feeling drunk and rowdy. She remembers the crisp air and stars shining bright up in the sky. She remembers looking at her friends and laughing.

Dr. Carlyle continues to guide Jenna. She watches as Jenna's face begins to contort and she's crying. Jenna starts to scream, "Help! Help! Why can't they see me? I'm over here. I'm going to die." Jenna starts to hyperventilate, and Dr. Carlyle quickly brings her out of her hypnotic state. Jenna looks at Dr. Carlyle. "Did I remember?"

Dr. Carlyle replied, “You tell me? Did you?”

Jenna leaned back and closed her eyes in frustration. “I feel like I remembered everything except for getting into the car.”

Dr. Carlyle looked over the notes she had been taking and replied, “It appears that you remembered everything up to when you took the Clonazepam and then you skipped over to when the Clonazepam wore off.”

Jenna let out a frustrated sigh and leaned her head back against the chair looking up at the ceiling. She could hear Dr. Carlyle talking about post-traumatic stress disorder then continued to explain about the effects of medication mixed with alcohol, but Jenna heard none of this. *How could she feel so sure that she was innocent but had no way to prove it?*

Dr. Carlyle suggested that maybe they should try again later but Jenna knew the results would be the same. She left the office and walked outside. She took out her phone and dialed Eric’s number. Right now, he seemed like her only friend. He answered on the second ring. Jenna smiled at the sound of his voice. “Hi, would you like to get a cup of coffee? I know this great little place.”

Eric laughed and said, “Would it happen to be the Java Cafe? I believe they also serve these amazing muffins too.”

Jenna laughed. “I’ve heard that. Are you free anytime soon?”

Eric replied, “You happen to have excellent timing. My shift ends in about ten minutes so what if I meet you in about half an hour?

"I'll see you then," Jenna said as she clicked off her phone.

The cafe wasn't very far from Dr. Carlyle's office, so she decided to walk. She breathed in the fresh air and felt the sun warming her skin. She took her time walking and thinking about her session with Dr. Carlyle hoping something would jar her memory. Nothing new was coming to mind. She was distracted when she heard a squeal from a little girl giggling as a squirrel raced across the sidewalk and grabbed a peanut that was lying on the sidewalk and then scampered up a tree. Jenna smiled and kept walking towards the cafe. She opened the door and stepped inside. The smell of coffee filled the air. It smelled amazing.

She ordered a large coffee and picked out a couple of muffins. She carried it to a small round table near a window. She had just taken a sip of her coffee when Eric walked through the door. He looked towards her and waved before walking to the counter to order his coffee. He sat down and looked at the muffins and laughed. Jenna looked at him and asked teasingly, "So did you rescue any damsels in distress today?"

Eric chuckled. "No, not much excitement. It was a quiet day. I like days like that. How is your day going?"

Jenna frowned. "I went to visit Dr. Carlyle today."

Eric looked up in surprise. "That was quick. How did it go?"

"Not the way I was hoping," Jenna replied.

Eric was quiet and looked at her sympathetically. She went to speak again but he interrupted. "Jenna, I could be called to testify against you. Maybe we should talk about other things."

Jenna shook her head, "It's okay. This is nothing new. I didn't remember."

"What?" Eric asked.

"I didn't remember. I know I didn't drive that night. I can feel it, but I can't prove it."

"Why don't you start at the beginning," Eric suggested.

"I remember all the way up to when I had the keys in my hand and then it skips over to when I was laying on the ground after the accident. I was really hoping I could remember so that we could investigate and prove that I'm innocent." Jenna sat back in frustration.

Eric grabbed a muffin and started peeling the paper away from it slowly. "Are you absolutely positive you weren't driving that night?"

Jenna ran a frustrated hand through her hair. "I swear, Eric, I don't remember getting behind that wheel and I just have a gut feeling that it wasn't me."

Eric studied her for a minute and then sighed. "Let me look into it. I'll see if I can find anything out."

Jenna shook her head. "I can't ask you to do that. This is my problem based on my own stupid decisions."

"I'm not breaking any rules and I'm not jeopardizing the case on either side. My job is to help people Jenna. Cops don't just run around looking for people to throw in jail."

Jenna thought for a minute. "I need all the help I can get according to my lawyer. If you can help that would be great. I'll do whatever you need me to."

Chapter 20
The Investigation

Eric walked into the office and headed straight to his partner's desk. He plopped a box of donuts down along with a large coffee and grinned at his partner John. John looked up and groaned, "You want a favor and I'm not going to like it."

Eric tried to look shocked. "John, I'm hurt. Here I just wanted to show some appreciation for the guy who always has my back and you think the worst."

John looked up at him. "Eric, we've known each other since we were kids. Hell, for a while you were my only friend. I know when I'm being set up."

Eric plopped into the chair next to John and picked up the box of donuts. He opened the lid and held out the box to John who couldn't resist. He picked up a chocolate covered donut and took a bite and moaned in pleasure. "Man," John said. "Claire is going to kill me. First for eating this and second for letting you tempt me. You know how she's always on me about my sugar."

Eric laughed. "What happens between brothers stays between brothers." Eric picked up a donut and then closed the lid. "Okay, you were right, I need a favor," said Eric taking a bite of the donut.

John grinned and took a sip of his coffee. "I knew it! Man, do I have you pegged."

Eric looked chagrined and then grew serious. "Do you remember that girl I saved in the car accident a few months ago?"

John leaned back in his chair and looked deep in thought, "That was the one where a girl died wasn't it? The other two girls were pretty banged up, right?"

Eric nodded. "That's the one."

John was all business. "What about it?"

Eric filled John in about the events of that night according to Jenna. When he finished the story he said, "The thing is man that I believe her. I don't know why, call it a hunch or a gut reaction, but I believe her."

John looked at his friend. "I get it. I'll look into it for you. Just do me a favor and don't get mixed up with this girl. You realize you were on the scene and you will be called to testify. Don't muddy the waters."

Eric slapped his hand on his friend's back. "No worries, you know me. I'm married to my job. I don't need any complications."

John laughed. "You say that now, but I remember that girl. She was attractive plus when you add a damsel in distress that's a cocktail for disaster."

Eric looked at his friend. “Attractive? Huh,” he said smiling, “I didn’t notice.” He stood up, grabbed another donut, and walked away as John shook his head and laughed.

Chapter 21
Kym

Kym stood nervously in front of the rickety old wooden door. She took a deep breath and knocked. She closed her eyes and said a silent prayer as the door creaked open and her mother stood in front of her. Kym smiled. "Hi, Mother."

Her mother's eyes grew wide with disbelief as she looked at her daughter. Kym stood trembling hoping she wouldn't be sent away. "Mom, are you okay?" She reached out and touched her mother. Kym could feel feeble bones where once a strong determined woman stood. Her mother held out her arms as Kym stepped into her embrace.

There was something so reassuring about being held in her mother's arms. Even though everything in Kym's life was crumbling down around her, being held by her mother made everything better somehow.

"Come in, come in." Her mother beckoned." How did you get here? What are you doing here? You didn't drop out of school, did you?"

Kym could see the worry starting to build in her mother's eyes and laughed. "No mother, I did not drop out of school. It is spring break. My friend Allie lent me the money to come and I came because I miss you and I worry about you."

Kym sat down at the little round table in the kitchen and watched her mother busy herself making tea. Kym stood up and took down two teacups from the cabinet. Her mother carried the tea kettle from the stove and sat it down between them. As they were steeping their tea her mother said quietly, "You know your father would be angry at you for wasting money coming here but I'm so happy to see you. I've missed you so much my daughter."

Kym's eyes welled with tears at the mention of her father. "I've missed you too." The two of them looked at each other leaving so much unsaid. Kym cleared her throat. "How is the market doing?"

Her mother pasted on a smile. "Business is good. We are very busy."

Kym knew her mother's smile wasn't genuine, but she also knew better than to question it. It would be a sign of disrespect, but she had her suspicions that things were not good financially. Kym took a sip of her tea. "Is Aunt Amelia still helping out?"

Her mother shook her head no and then before Kym could ask any more questions her mother interrupted, "How is everything back in the United States? What is it like there? I want to hear everything."

Kym shifted uncomfortably in her seat. "Well, I have sent you tons of pictures so that you can see for yourself."

Her mother shook her head. "No, what I mean is do you like living there?"

This was Kym's chance to come clean and tell her mother that she wanted to stay. She opened her mouth to tell her that but saw the hope reflected in her mother's eyes and knew she couldn't hurt her that way. Kym smiled and said, "Yes, mother it is a wonderful place to live." Kym changed the subject quickly. "Allie is great. Like I said earlier, she lent me the money to come visit. She's a great friend and helped me a lot when Father passed away."

Her mother pressed on. "How are your other friends?"

Kym swallowed a lump in her throat and hoped she wouldn't burst into tears. "They are fine. We all get along well and help each other." Kym stood up and yawned. "It's been a long two days and I'm really tired. I'd like to get some rest and then maybe we can go to the market?"

She noted the surprise on her mother's face. "Sure," Mother replied. "Go lie down and get some rest."

Kym walked through her childhood home towards her bedroom. It was exactly how she had left it. She slipped off her shoes and crawled into bed. She knew she wouldn't sleep. She hadn't slept much since the accident. Every time she closed her eyes the nightmares would start. She would hear Cara groaning, she could feel the panic welling up inside her, and then she would wake up drenched with sweat and screaming.

Kym pulled up the delicate bedspread that her grandmother had made for her sixteenth birthday. It gave her comfort to have the things she cherished most around her. She closed her eyes thinking of her mother and the market. Something was not right she could feel it. Her mother looked so frail and her face was creased with worry. Kym knew her mother was determined to follow "the plan" that her father had devised so many years ago.

Kym looked at the clock on her nightstand and saw that it was twelve o'clock. She sat up with a start. She had forgotten about the time change between China and New York. Her mother should have been at the market hours ago. Her parents were usually there at sunup to start setting out their produce. Kym folded up her blanket and padded out to the kitchen. The house was quiet, and Kym noticed a note on the table:

Dearest Kym,

I didn't want to wake you. I went to the market to work and then I will be home. You have traveled a long way and must surely be tired. I have made up a plate of food for when you get hungry. I will be home later. Take this time to rest and relax.

Love,

Mother

Kym opened the refrigerator and pulled out a dish of Liang Cai. She uncovered the plate wrapped in plastic wrap and grabbed a set of chopsticks. She dug into the luscious vegetables and tofu. This was one of her favorite dishes and she relished in the authentic spices and sauce of the dish. She had missed this.

Once she had eaten, she washed her dish and put it away. She slipped on her shoes and was glad she was close enough to walk to the Market Square. Kym stepped out of the tiny house and closed the door behind her. She slipped a pink baseball cap over her head to shade her face from the sun.

Kym stopped by the first vendor and bought some flowers to take with her to the cemetery. "Kym, you're home!" said Mrs. Huang coming around her vendor cart and giving Kym a hug. "Your mother must be thrilled!"

Kym smiled back at her mother's long-time friend. "Yes, she is happy. How is business?"

Mrs. Huang lowered her voice in a conspiratorial tone, "Business hasn't been so good since your father passed."

Kym was confused. "What does my father's passing have to do with your business?"

Mrs. Huang shook her head. "Not my business, dear. I was talking about your parents' business, but surely you already know all about it." Mrs. Huang pulled Kym towards her in another hug. "I'm so glad you came back to help your mother."

Kym kissed the woman's cheek and wished her well as she continued to her family's produce stand. She could see the bright rainbow-colored awning over the produce stand. Kym walked up to the stand in stunned disbelief. Most of the tables were empty and the produce that remained was either overripe or bruised. She looked for her mother and found her in the back room. "Mother? What is going on?" Kym asked quietly walking into the little room.

Her mother jumped at the sound of Kym's voice. "Kym, I thought you would stay home and relax. What are you doing here?"

Kym looked around and asked, "Mother, why are you sitting back here? Where is all the produce? What is going on?"

Her mother forced a smile. "It was a busy day! We've sold nearly everything. I'm just sitting down resting."

Kym pulled a chair over to her mother and sat down. She took her mother's hand in hers. "Mother, I can see that the market is in trouble. I can help. I'm not a little girl anymore." Kym watched her mother wipe away the tears that trickled down her face and waited for her mother to speak.

"It's been so hard, Kym. Since your father passed, things have been so hard. I tried to keep up with everything. I really did, but the produce is heavy for me and I sometimes drop the boxes which bruises the fruits and vegetables. I try to keep the books, but I was never very good at that. Numbers have always been you and your father's passion. I fell behind in paying the vendors and had to use the business as collateral for a loan to pay for the funeral expenses."

Kym cried along with her mother as she listened. "The bank is foreclosing on the market," her mother finally whispered.

Kym stood up. "Wow, I knew things would be hard adjusting to not having Father here but I never dreamed this would happen. Didn't Father have a life insurance policy to help with expenses?"

Her mother nodded. "Yes," she whispered, "But we cashed it in to send you to America and to pay for your tuition."

"What?" Kym asked in disbelief. "Father told me it was all taken care of. He said everything was paid for through grants."

Mother smiled. "He didn't want you to worry or feel guilty. You are our only hope for a better life."

Kym looked panic stricken. *This can't be happening!*

Kym stood up and looked around. "We'll fix this. I can help you fix this. I'll straighten out the books. I'll unload the produce. I will work here with you. We can fix this."

Kym's mother shook her head. "No, Kym it's too late. Last week I signed the paperwork to give the market back to the bank. I can't afford to pay the vendors but luckily they are letting me pay a little at a time."

Kym stood up and started straightening up the desk and organizing papers. "No, mother I am going to fix this!"

Her mother stood up and put a hand on Kym's arm. "Honey, it is going to be okay. We were going to sell the market anyway. You are graduating soon, and I will be moving away from here. None of this matters anymore."

Kym began to feel physically sick. "Mother, I..."

"I heard you were home!" Kym turned around to see Chao standing in the doorway smiling at her.

"Chao!" Kym exclaimed as she walked over and hugged him close to her. "I've missed you so much!"

Chao whispered back, "I've missed you too."

Kym's mother stood up. "I'll let the two of you catch up. We'll talk later, okay?"

Kym's heart sank as she turned towards her mother. "Yes, we'll talk later."

Chao took Kym by the hand as they walked through the Market Square. Kym stopped to chat and hug vendors that she had known all her life. Chao led her away from the market and towards a gravel path that would lead them down by the river. As they walked hand in hand Kym felt truly at home and felt a peaceful feeling of belonging, one she hasn't felt in a very long time. They stopped by the river's edge and perched on their favorite boulder. Chao leaned in and kissed Kym. It began tentatively but then Kym could feel the desire building up with each flick of their tongues. She wrapped her arms around him and let the kiss consume her. Nothing else mattered except being here, right now, with Chao. He was her future. He was the one she loved.

Chao pulled away and looked into her eyes. "I have something for you."

She smiled mischievously. "You do?"

Chao reached into his pocket and pulled out a small box. He opened it and said, "Will you be my wife? Will you marry me?"

She stared at the ring and then at him. "Yes! Yes, I will marry you!"

Chao took the ring out of the box and slipped it on her finger. "It's a perfect fit," Chao said. "Just like us."

Kym gazed at the ring. "It is beautiful. I can't believe this is happening. How did you get my family's permission?"

Chao winced. "I didn't." Kym started to say something, but Chao continued before she could. "Kym, I love you. Your father had already passed. We are both adults. We know what we want." He stood up and looked out at the river. "We don't need anyone's permission to marry. We only need each other. I have a good job. I can support you. I've been saving up for a house."

Kym was silent for a moment and then looked down at the ring. "I do love you Chao and I do want to be your wife." She took a deep breath and continued, "I just got back here, and my mother still expects me to go back to the United States to finish my classes. She still has that plan for me to move her back there with me. How can I disappoint her when I know how hard she is struggling?"

Chao responded gently, "How can you not stay when you know how hard she is struggling?"

Kym frowned, he didn't know that her mother just sold the market and all of their money had gone towards sending her to college.

Chao blew out an exasperated breath. "Let's not worry about this now. We'll work it out. The important thing is that we are spending our life together."

Kym smiled and leaned in to give him another kiss. "You're right and I can't wait to marry you."

Chapter 22
Decisions

The house was dark and quiet when Kym let herself in. She walked over to a small table and turned on the lamp. She quietly walked down to the far room at the end of the hallway. Kym saw her mother sleeping peacefully on the bed. She looked small and so much older.

Kym sat down at a small desk and turned on the laptop. She typed the name Jenna Lewis into the search engine to see if there was any more news about her friend. She had not been allowed to contact Jenna before she left and she was worried about her.

Kym sifted through many different articles from local newspapers all saying the same thing. Jenna had been arrested and was about to go to trial for the murder of Cara Donnelly. Kym didn't understand the American legal system but knew that Cara's death had been an accident not murder. Kym had even said so when she gave her statement to the police. She stared at the photo of Jenna taken at the police station. Jenna looked awful.

Kym's cell phone began to ring, and she quickly answered it so as to not wake her mother. She looked at the screen and didn't recognize the number.

"Hello?" she said tentatively.

"May I speak with Miss Kym Syndako?" a voice on the other end said.

"You are speaking with her," Kym replied feeling her stomach clench.

"Miss Syndako, this is Officer Lawrence, from the Evanston Police Department. I was calling in reference to the accident that you were involved in on March 25, 2016."

Kym's knees were starting to shake, she sat down on the edge of the chair. "I already gave my statement," she replied.

"Yes, ma'am you did. I had a few follow up questions to ask you and wondered if we could meet on Monday at one o'clock?" inquired Officer Lawrence.

Kym was quiet for a moment and then spoke, "I'm afraid that isn't possible. I am in China visiting my mother. My father just recently passed, and I was needed at home." Kym could hear the clicking of computer keys as the officer was typing something in.

"Miss Syndako, are you aware that this is an ongoing investigation and that you were not allowed to leave the country?"

Kym's heart stopped, and she was having difficulty breathing. "No, I didn't. I had given my statement and I have cooperated with the authorities. I apologize for not telling you that I had to fly home on a family emergency."

The officer was quiet for a moment and then said, "Miss Syndako, the trial for Jenna Lewis is on August seventeenth starting at eight a.m. The prosecutor would like for you to be a witness for the state. It is imperative that you are at the trial in order to corroborate the evidence being presented against the defendant."

Kym's breath hitched. "Officer I don't mean any disrespect, but I am unable to leave at the moment. My mother needs me here."

Kym could hear more keys clicking and then Officer Lawrence said, "Miss Syndako, you have already broken the law by leaving the country; if I notify the state of this information your visa will be revoked. I suggest you pick up the ticket that I will reserve for you at the airport and be in my office Monday afternoon at one o'clock."

Kym dropped her phone back into her purse as her mother came walking into the living room. "Was that one of your roommates dear?"

Kym tried to smile. "Yes, I called Allie to tell her that I had arrived safely."

Her mother started heating up the tea kettle. "I'm glad you have such caring friends." Her mother took down two tea cups and placed them on the table.

Kym stood up from her seat and said, "I think I'll go for a walk. You just relax and enjoy your tea. I bought some flowers earlier to place on Father's grave. I'd like to do that before they wilt. I'll be back soon." Kym walked over and kissed her mother on the cheek.

Kym left the house and started walking towards the cemetery. She still desperately missed her father. Her thumb rubbed across the back of the ring that Chao had given her. She hoped that her father would have approved. She also knew in her heart that she belonged here. She didn't want to be a disgrace and she hoped her mother would understand.

Kym walked over to the burial plot that was still covered with dirt. She sat down on the ground as her eyes filled with tears. Thoughts of her childhood ran through her mind. She smiled wistfully as she remembered the mischievous look in her father's eyes when he gave her a gift for her sixteenth birthday. She remembered opening the box to find nothing there and how everyone had laughed and laughed, then her father held up a beautiful necklace and placed it around her neck.

Her mind drifted to her mother and all those nights in the kitchen where she had learned to cook. How they would both laugh at the mess they left behind. There had been so much laughter in her childhood and so much love. She had focused so much on herself and resented the stress of disappointing everyone around her that she forgot the most important lesson her parents had taught her. She was a strong, independent, proud Chinese woman.

She stood up and dusted off the bits of grass and dirt that were on her clothes. She took a deep breath and looked up at the clear blue sky. She finally felt in control of her life for the first time in a very long time. She knew what she had to do to fix all of this.

She reached into her purse and pulled out her cell phone. She dialed the number she was looking for.

"Hello, this is Officer Lawrence how may I help you?"

Kym took a big breath and said, "Officer Lawrence this is Kym Syndako, you can expect me at our appointed time on Monday. I am going to the airport now to pick up my ticket and I expect it to be ready when I get there." She hung up before Officer Lawrence had a chance to reply.

Next, she walked home with a purpose. Today was only Thursday which gave her plenty of time to put her plan in action. She walked through the door and saw her mother resting on the couch. "Hi Mother, are you feeling okay?" Kym asked tentatively.

Her mother smiled. "Yes, I am fine. I'm just a little tired that's all."

Kym sat next to her and hugged her. "I was thinking that perhaps tomorrow we can enjoy a day out together. Do you think you are up to that?"

Her mother nodded and looked at her daughter. "I am so glad you are home."

Kym smiled wistfully. "Me too." She watched as her mother drifted back to sleep and then she picked up the keys to the car.

She drove to the airport and cashed in her return ticket and pocketed the money. She walked over to another desk and picked up the ticket that Officer Lawrence had waiting for her then she returned to her car. She looked at the ticket sitting in her hand and ripped it in half. She was in control now and she had no intention of going back.

Next, she pulled out her cell phone and dialed Chao's number. "Hello, my beautiful soon to be bride," Chao answered.

Kym laughed. "Hello, my one and only love. Can I see you? There is something I want to tell you and it can't wait until tomorrow."

"This sounds mysterious. You're not thinking of breaking off the engagement, are you?" Chao asked suddenly concerned.

"No, it's not that at all. It's something else. I will be there in about ten minutes. I love you," Kym said as she hung up the phone.

Ten minutes later Kym pulled up in front of Chao's house. He met her on the doorstep as she walked up. Chao pulled Kym towards him and kissed her. She felt dizzy when the kiss ended. He sat down on the stoop and wrapped his arms around her. "Okay, lady of my life what is this news that cannot wait?"

Kym took a deep breath and explained to Chao about the bank taking the market and how her mother would not have any source of income. "Chao, this market has been in my family for three generations. We can't lose it!" Chao had a feeling he knew what was coming. Kym looked up at Chao earnestly. "You said that you had been saving money for a house. Please, please can we use it to buy back the market instead?"

Chao was quiet as he looked at Kym. Her face was contorted with all the pain she had been carrying inside. He knew he didn't have much choice. "I will give you the money on one condition," Chao said.

"I will agree to any condition," Kym said quickly.

Chao took a deep breath not knowing how Kym would react. "That you will stay in China with me."

Kym smiled and said, "I agree. I know that I belong here." Kym looked up into his eyes. "Can I ask for one more favor?"

Chao threw his head back and laughed. "Woman you are making me insane. What is it?"

Kym looked serious. "Can we go to the bank tomorrow and sign the papers? Tomorrow is Friday and I would like to surprise my mother on Saturday."

Chao leaned down and kissed Kym. "Yes, my darling, irresistible, impulsive woman, we will go to the bank first thing tomorrow morning."

Chapter 23
Kym's Plan

The next morning Kym jumped out of bed and walked into the kitchen. Her mother smiled at her. "You're looking very happy this morning."

Kym walked over and gave her mother a kiss on the cheek. "I am very happy this morning. How can I not be when I wake up and smell your amazing cooking?" Her mother laughed.

Kym poured herself a cup of tea and then looked at her mother. "I was thinking of visiting Chao this morning if that is okay."

Her mother smiled and said, "Of course, just remember don't get attached. You are going back to class."

Kym felt guilty for hiding her engagement and her intentions from her mother, but she knew in the end it would be worth it.

The two women sat at the table and started eating. Kym looked at her mother. "What are your plans for today?"

Her mother frowned. "I will be at the market. I have to finish cleaning it up for the bank and sorting through all the finances."

Kym looked at her mother. "How about if I come to the market a little later and I will take care of all the bookwork for you. I might even help you clean," she added teasingly.

Her mother looked relieved. "I would love that. I'm fine with cleaning but all those numbers are foreign to me."

Kym stood up and put her plate into the sink. "I will be there as soon as I can," she promised.

Kym met Chao at the bank and hugged him tightly. "Thank you for doing this."

Chao kissed the top of her head. "No thanks needed, my love. I will always take care of your family."

Kym looked up at him. "Promise?" she asked tentatively.

He looked down at her solemnly. "I promise."

Kym left the bank a short time later and went straight to the market. She found her mother looking tired and overwhelmed. Kym smiled and said jokingly, "Don't worry mother reinforcements are here."

Her mother looked up and smiled. "Thank goodness!"

Kym was bursting to tell her mother the good news but knew that she had to be patient. Tomorrow would come soon enough.

The alarm woke Kym the next morning. She could smell breakfast cooking and was excited to start the day. She had made reservations for lunch at the Grand Hotel. Kym remembered sitting in the back seat of the car as a small child and watching her father reach over and hold her mother's hand. He had driven past the Grand Hotel and he had said, "One day, I will take you there." Kym had been touched by the adoring look her father had given her mother. She knew it was expensive and to her knowledge they had never been able to afford to go there.

The two women ate breakfast silently both lost in their own thoughts. Once they had finished eating Kym offered to clean up while her mother got dressed. Kym had planned a whole day of sightseeing at all of their favorite places and then they would go to lunch.

"Are you ready?" Kym asked her mother excitedly.

Her mother laughed. "Where are we going?"

"You'll find out," Kym said grinning.

The two women climbed in the car as Kym began their adventure. Kym drove to a park that she had often visited as a child. The two women sat on the bench telling stories of the past. Sometimes they would laugh and other times they would wipe a tear away from the corner of their eye. Each stop led them closer to the Grand Hotel and when Kym finally pulled up in front of the hotel and handed the valet her keys her mother looked at her in astonishment. "Kym, we can't go there. It's much too expensive."

Kym smiled widely at her mother and said, "Yes, we are going there. We have reservations. Now, let's get out of the car and go inside."

Kym's mother looked at her daughter as her eyes filled with tears. "Your father had always said he would bring me here one day."

Kym's eyes filled with tears. "I know. I am keeping his promise."

Kym and her mother walked into the Grand Hotel with their arms linked. They checked their coats in and were shown to their table. The dining hall looked like a ballroom with glorious crystal chandeliers hanging from the ceiling and meals served on silver trays. There were fresh flowers on every table with a candle lit in the center. Their host pulled out her mother's chair for her and helped her to get situated. Kym smiled and handed her mother a menu. Her mother giggled. "I can't believe that I am here." She put her menu down and looked at her daughter. "Thank you," she said wiping away a single tear.

After dinner Kym insisted that they order dessert and hot tea. "I don't think I have room for anything else," her mother protested.

Kym laughed and said, "Yes, you do because we're celebrating."

Her mother looked at her quizzically, "What are we celebrating?"

Kym's whole face glowed with anticipation as she reached into her purse and handed her mother the papers.

Her mother took them and said, "What is this?"

Kym's heart burst with love for her mother. "It is paperwork that says that the market is yours."

Her mother held her hand to her chest and looked up at Kym shocked. "But how?"

Kym knew her mother was a proud woman and would not take handouts. "Chao helped me to purchase it. I am technically the owner, but I am giving it to you. It is a gift for all the sacrifices you and father have made for me."

Her mother suddenly looked ten years younger. She stood up and kissed her daughter and hugged her tight. "Thank you, Kym! I just can't believe it!"

Later that night, Kym drove to Chao's house. She smiled widely as she told him about her mother's reaction. She kissed him lightly on the lips and said, "Thank you again."

Chao kissed her back but this time a little more passionately. They wrapped themselves up in each other as they kissed then Kym began to unbutton Chao's shirt. He stopped and looked at her in surprise. Kym smiled and then kissed him again. "Make love to me. I know we were going to wait but I can't any longer. I love you so much, Chao, and I want you to love all of me."

Chao looked into Kym's eyes and saw the smoldering passion reflected back at him. He knew he should wait but the time felt so right. He lifted her from the couch and carried her to his bed. He gently laid her down and asked one more time, "Are you sure?"

Her heart skipped a beat and she was nervous, but she smiled. "More than sure. I love you."

The next morning was Sunday and Kym smiled thinking of the night before. She was so amazingly happy and knew that everything had worked out perfectly so far. She walked into the kitchen and saw the note on the table:

> Kym,
>
> I went to the market to place the orders and start setting up. I still can't believe you did this. Thank you so much and I love you more than you know.
>
> Love,
>
> Mom

Kym smiled and put the note back down on the table. Today was the day to put the last part of her plan in action. She put on her running shoes and tied her hair in a ponytail. She stepped outside into the glorious day and began jogging towards the bluff overlooking the river.

Chapter 24
August 19, 2016

Jenna sat nervously at the table in front of the courtroom. She could feel herself sweating and was sure she would throw up any minute. Her parents were seated behind her and Mark was reviewing his opening statement. Jenna's knee was bouncing up and down and she was trying to take deep breaths to calm her racing heart.

She jumped when she felt a hand on her shoulder. She turned her head to see her dad squeezing her shoulder reassuringly. "It'll be okay. Whatever happens, we'll get through it."

Jenna tried to smile and caught her breath as her eyes roamed past her father towards the back of the courtroom. Allie was sitting on a bench looking straight at her. *Did she think I was guilty? Why was she here?* Jenna didn't have time to think about it as the bailiff walked into the courtroom and announced, "Please rise for the Honorable Judge Wilcox."

Everyone stood. The judge entered the courtroom and said, “You may be seated.” He proceeded to read through the charges and Jenna could hear a woman sobbing behind her. Jenna’s heart sank as she thought of all the people she had brought sadness to...her family, Cara’s family, Cara’s friends.

The room felt like it was spinning, and Jenna began to see dark spots. She tried taking deep breaths as Mark leaned over and whispered in her ear, “Don’t worry. Remember the prosecutor must prove their case beyond a reasonable doubt.” He picked up his notes and turned to walk towards the jury.

“Ladies and gentlemen of the jury, my name is Mark Davis and I am representing the defendant Jenna Lewis.”

Jenna could feel all of the jurors’ eyes boring through her. It felt like she had already been given the verdict of guilty. She tried to meet their eyes, as Mark had instructed her to, but she knew that at any second she was going to be sick. She turned her head away from the jury and tried to concentrate on her breathing.

“Jenna is a law student at McClellan University. She is a typical student not unlike many other students from the university. She shared a house with her roommates Kym Syndako, Cara Donnelly, and Allie Stratford. All of the girls got along great and were the best of friends. They supported one another and were there for each other which is how Jenna, on the evening of March twenty-fifth, found herself involved in a train of events that were beyond her control.

"On the afternoon of March twenty-fifth Jenna came home from her law class to discover that her friend, Kym Syndako, had just found out that her father had passed away from a fatal heart attack. Kym was understandably upset, and Jenna had gone to Kym's room to comfort her friend. While the two girls were talking, Cara Donnelly entered the room along with Allie Stratford. Allie was the one who suggested going out to the local pub and all the girls agreed. The intention wasn't to drink themselves into inebriation but instead to help their friend Kym celebrate her father's life rather than mourn her father's death. The four girls walked into Mulcahey's Pub, a common hangout for college students, and ordered some drinks as typical students do.

"While Jenna was trying to be supportive and help Kym through this difficult time she also learned that her best friend Cara was upset about an ongoing relationship. All of these young ladies left the establishment together to confront the gentleman in question. They reached his house and an altercation ensued. The girls left peacefully with Cara driving the car. Cara was feeling ill and pulled the car over. Allie received a phone call from a friend and took the keys from Cara and drove everyone to Mickey's Hideout to meet up with her friends.

"At approximately two a.m. Jenna, trying to be the voice of reason, tried coaxing Kym and Cara to leave the bar. Allie had decided to stay behind with her friend. All three girls left the establishment together. As they were driving home it began to rain heavily. Unfortunately, the combination of heavy rain, slippery roads, and a driver who may or may not have been intoxicated all contributed to the accident that resulted in the death of Cara Donnelly.

"The prosecution will try and convince you that Jenna was under the influence of prescription drugs and alcohol. However, Jenna had recently been diagnosed with a bi-polar disorder and was taking a prescribed medication. Something responsible people do to neutralize this disorder. Jenna has no recollection of driving the car during the time of the accident. It is the burden of proof by the prosecution to prove *beyond a reasonable doubt* that Jenna was the person responsible for the death of her best friend Cara Donnelly."

The jurors looked over at Jenna who was dabbing her eyes with a tissue. Mark turned towards Jenna and walked over to her putting his arm around her to console her, hoping this will tug at the jurors' heart strings. Mark looked back at the jury. "We have no proof that Jenna was the driver of that vehicle. Jenna has no recollection of driving the car at any point that night. There is only speculation and hearsay in this case. I ask the jury to keep this in mind while listening to the testimony. Thank you."

The judge cleared his throat and declared, "The prosecutor, Miss Thomason may now make her opening statement."

A woman stood up and adjusted her jacket. "Thank you, Your Honor." She strode confidently towards the jury and began to speak. "Ladies and gentlemen of the jury, you are here to decide the fate of the defendant, Jenna Lewis. The defense would like you to believe that Jenna is a responsible young adult who had the best interest of her friends at heart.

That perhaps *she* is the victim. What the defense is not telling you and what you will discover in the testimony is that Jenna is not the person that Mr. Davis has depicted her to be. She abused prescription drugs which is a common problem in our society today. Responsible people know when to stop drinking. The combination of the drugs in Jenna's system and her excessive drinking resulted in the death of Cara Donnelly.

"Cara is the victim here, not Jenna. Cara was on her way to becoming an excellent nurse. She was completing her last semester in college and then she would have graduated. She undoubtedly would have done great things with her life if it were not cut short through no fault of her own. *Cara* is the victim in all this. Cara, who was always smiling, always helping, who was on the Dean's list and moving up in life. Cara, who was a daughter, a sister, a friend, a person everyone genuinely loved to be around. Cara, who was killed by the irresponsible acts of the defendant. The state is confident that upon hearing all the evidence, you will agree that Jenna Lewis is guilty of second degree manslaughter in the death of Cara Donnelly."

There was complete silence in the courtroom except for the occasional soft sob coming from Cara's family members. Once again Jenna could feel all eyes staring accusingly at her. She wanted to scream, "I'M INNOCENT!" but was she? Could she truly and positively say without a doubt that she wasn't the driver?

The prosecutor's piercing blue eyes looked smugly at Jenna as she walked over to her table, pulled out her chair, and sat down.

The judge cleared his throat and said, "The prosecution may call its first witness."

Jenna sat rigid feeling sick to her stomach as the prosecution called person after person up to the stand. She listened as her whole life went on display for all of these strangers. She listened as every mistake she'd ever made was brought to light. She listened mutely as the prosecutor delved into her brushes with the law as a juvenile, her low grades and truancy, her drinking and partying as a teen, and her rebellious relationship with her parents.

Next, the prosecution called Officer Eric Copeland to the stand. Jenna watched as he was sworn in and then sat down. He wouldn't look at Jenna but instead looked directly at the prosecutor as she began to proceed. "Officer Copeland, you were called to an accident on the night of March twenty-fifth, 2016 is that correct?"

Eric replied, "Yes, that is correct."

The prosecutor continued, "Can you tell the court what transpired that night?"

Eric shifted in his seat. "At approximately three a.m. Saturday morning a 911 call came through reporting an accident on Route 28A. We immediately dispatched an ambulance, fire truck, and two police vehicles to the scene. When we arrived, we discovered a vehicle had rolled over and was lying upside down on the pavement. It was raining very hard and it was difficult to see. We looked inside the vehicle and spotted an unconscious female in the front passenger seat. The fire department used the Jaws of Life to extract her from the vehicle. The paramedics arrived and placed her on the ground but, unfortunately, they could not find any vitals. They tried to resuscitate her but were unsuccessful. She was pronounced dead at the scene."

Jenna could hear a moan coming from the courtroom and without looking knew it was Cara's mother. Jenna began to shake as she flashed back to that night. She remembered how she felt as the freezing rain pelted her skin while she lay on the hard ground. She could still hear the wail of sirens and frantic shouting of the paramedics and policemen. She remembered the fear she felt when she was sure she was going to die.

"Was the female victim you are referring to Cara Donnelly?" the prosecutor asked.

Eric cleared his throat. "Yes, it was."

"What else did you discover at the scene, Officer Copeland?"

"My partner discovered another female victim that had been ejected from the car and was sitting dazed in the road approximately 15 feet from the vehicle."

"Who was this female later identified as?" the prosecutor asked looking at the jury.

Eric continued, "Kym Syndako."

"Were there any other victims at the scene?" the prosecutor asked.

Eric looked briefly at Jenna then back to the prosecutor. "Yes, Jenna Lewis."

The prosecution waited for Eric to continue but he remained silent. The prosecutor continued, "Judge Wilcox, I would like to introduce into evidence, Exhibit A." Within seconds two court clerks carried in the diagram depicting the scene of the accident. The prosecution pulled out a pointer and asked Eric, "Could you please point out where you found Jenna Lewis?"

Eric stood and walked towards the diagram. He used the pointer to show the court where he had discovered Jenna's body.

Jenna's mind flashed back to the relief she felt when she saw Eric looking down on her in the pouring rain and telling her everything was going to be okay.

The prosecutor continued, "In your expert opinion, Officer Copeland, would Jenna's location in comparison to the car be conducive to the location of where the driver of the vehicle could have been?"

Eric directed his steely eyes on the prosecutor. "It's possible."

The prosecutor smiled smugly and said, "No further questions Your Honor."

Mark stood and walked towards the witness stand. "Officer Copeland, you stated that it was possible that my client could have been the driver, is that correct."

"Yes," Eric replied.

"In your opinion, could it also be possible that someone else could have been driving the car? Perhaps Miss Syndako?"

Eric avoided Jenna's eyes. "From the evidence at the scene based on the positions of all people involved it seems most likely that Miss Lewis may have been in the driver's seat, Cara located in the front passenger seat, and Kym seated behind Cara."

Mark looked at the jury. "You said, 'most likely' does that mean that you can't definitively say without a doubt that Jenna was the one driving that night?"

Eric looked at the jury. "No, sir, I cannot."

Mark continued, "How was the condition of my client when you located her?"

Eric responded, "She was disorientated and drifting in and out of consciousness. It also appeared that she was physically injured but the First Responders at the scene were the ones to examine her."

"Did Miss Lewis ever admit that she was driving the vehicle?"

"No, she did not."

"Your Honor, I'd like to admit into evidence the statement that was written by Miss Lewis soon after the accident." Mark handed a copy to both the judge and Eric.

"Mr. Copeland, is there anywhere in this statement a confession from Jenna that she was driving the vehicle?"

"No, there is not," Eric replied.

Mark continued, "What exactly did she say?"

Eric responded, "She said that she did not remember."

Mark looked over at Jenna then back at Eric. "Has my client been cooperative during this investigation?"

"Yes, she has," Eric replied.

"To your knowledge has she sought other avenues to help her recover her memory?" Mark questioned.

Eric looked at Jenna. "To my knowledge, she has taken a polygraph and has also sought out a hypnotist."

Marked looked from Eric to the jury. "Were these things that she was ordered to do?"

Eric shook his head. "She was ordered to take a polygraph which came back inconclusive. I had made a suggestion about seeing a hypnotist because I know cases in which it has helped. Jenna was the one who made the final decision to make an appointment and go."

Mark looked at the judge. "No, more questions, Your Honor."

Mark then called Dr. Carlyle to the stand. "Dr. Carlyle, can you please state for the jury your credentials please?"

"I am a board certified clinical hypnotherapist. I also have a doctoral degree in psychology," Dr. Carlyle stated.

"Objection, Your Honor," the prosecutor shouted. "Hypnotism is not admissible in a court of law."

"Sustained," replied Judge Wilcox.

Mark looked at the judge. "Your Honor, I am simply trying to prove that Miss Lewis did indeed explore avenues to help her remember if she was the driver of the car."

The judge eyed Mark skeptically. "I'll allow you to continue Mr. Davis with a reminder to the jury that hypnosis is not admissible evidence."

Mark approached the witness stand as he continued his questioning. "Did you have an appointment with Miss Lewis on June the second, 2016?"

"Yes, I did," replied Dr. Carlyle. "She said that she wanted to try to remember what had happened on the night of the accident."

"Did you have any success?" Mark asked.

"Unfortunately, no," Dr. Carlyle replied.

"Can you explain to the court some of the reasons which may have attributed to Miss Lewis not being able recall this information?"

Dr. Carlyle responded, "Hypnotherapy doesn't work for everyone. Your mind must be in a state where it is very open to suggestion. It is not the be-all and end-all but it may trigger something that will guide you in the right direction. Unfortunately, in Miss Lewis's case, the memory may be more suppressed or perhaps the right questions weren't being asked."

"Thank you, Dr. Carlyle. No further questions," Mark said confidently as he walked back towards his table.

The prosecutor stood up. "Dr. Carlyle, can you please explain to the court what the average number of visits one would have when seeking the help of a hypnotherapist?"

Dr. Carlyle looks at the prosecutor. "It's hard to say. Many of my clients come in weekly. It depends on the client."

The prosecutor turns towards the jury. "You had stated that Miss Lewis was unsuccessful at remembering the events of the accident, is that correct?"

"Yes, that is correct," stated Dr. Carlyle confidently.

"Did you suggest another appointment?" asked the prosecutor.

"I did," replied Dr. Carlyle.

"What was her response?"

Dr. Carlyle looked at the prosecutor. "She declined."

The prosecutor nodded her head and replied, "No further questions."

Dr. Carlyle stepped out of the witness stand and Mark called his next witness. "I would like to call Dr. Woo to the stand."

Dr. Woo walked towards the bailiff and was sworn in, then he took the witness stand. Mark walked up to him and said, "Can you please state your occupation and your relationship to the defendant?"

Dr. Woo looked at the jury and said, "I am a primary care doctor at the Universal Clinic and Jenna Lewis is a patient of mine."

"Can you explain to the court what you have determined Jenna's medical condition to be?"

The doctor looked at the jury and stated, "Jenna has consented to let me discuss her case with you. After some testing it was decided that Jenna suffers from a bipolar disorder. I have prescribed medications that will help her to balance her mood swings."

Mark continued with his questioning. "Dr. Woo, when you prescribed Miss Lewis Lithium and Clonazepam, did you instruct her on the possible hazards of over medicating or mixing her medication with alcohol?"

Dr. Woo responded, "Yes, I always want my patients to be as knowledgeable as possible about the side effects or dangers of a particular medication. I explained to Jenna that common side effects from using Lithium may include; feeling tired, drowsiness, poor concentration, and memory problems. She was also told that this medication cannot be mixed with alcohol. Clonazepam has many of the same side effects."

Mark redirected the questioning. "Was this medication helping Jenna to overcome some of the obstacles of her bipolar disorder and panic attacks?"

Dr. Mason replied, "Yes, it was extremely effective, and Miss Lewis was exhibiting great success with them."

"Thank you Dr.Woo. That will be all for this witness, Your Honor," Mark announced.

The prosecutor stood up and began to question Dr.Woo. "You stated that you explained to Jenna the effects of mixing alcohol and her medication?"

"That is correct," Dr. Woo replied.

"Did Miss Lewis understand the instructions that you were giving her?"

"Yes, we did medical checks every three months to make sure that the medication was working and to answer any questions or concerns Miss Lewis may have."

"In your expert opinion, Dr. Woo," the prosecutor said, "Is it possible that an effect from binge drinking and a mixture of medication could have resulted in Miss Lewis's lapse in memory?"

"Yes," Dr. Mason replied.

"Would it be possible that Jenna would still be conscious enough to drive a vehicle?"

"Yes, she could have been."

The prosecutor looked at Jenna. "No further questions for this witness, Your Honor. The prosecution would like to call Allie Stratford to the stand."

Jenna couldn't breathe. Why Allie? She wasn't even a part of this. Jenna looked quizzically at Mark, but he was too busy making notes to notice. Jenna sat rigidly in her seat wondering what Allie could possibly say about her.

The prosecutor wasted no time before approaching the witness. "Were you with the defendant on the night of March twenty-fifth, 2016?"

Jenna could see that Allie was nervous. "Yes, I was," she replied not looking at Jenna.

"Can you recount the events that led up to Miss Lewis leaving Mickey's Hideout on March twenty-fifth, 2016?"

Allie retold her recollection of that night. She wiped her eyes as she explained how Kym's father had passed away from a heart attack and how Kym was not allowed to fly home to her family. She twisted a tissue in her hand when she explained how all the girls supported one another and had decided to go to Mulcahey's Pub to celebrate Kym's father's zest for life instead of his passing. She continued detailing Cara's troubled relationship with Trent and how he had cheated on her. She spoke about Cara driving erratically from Trent's house and how they convinced Cara to pull over. She confessed that Jeff had called and wanted the girls to meet him at Mickey's Hideout and that they had agreed to go. Allie explained how she had decided to stay with Jeff that night instead of leaving with her friends. Jenna could see the guilt on Allie's face for not going with them that night.

The prosecutor continued her questioning. "As the girls were leaving did you see Miss Lewis pull out her keys to drive that night?"

Allie avoided Jenna's eyes and looked down. "Yes."

"Did you do anything to try and stop her?" the prosecutor asked.

Allie choked back a sob. "No, I didn't. If I had then maybe none of this would have happened."

"No further questions, Your Honor."

The judge looked at the prosecutor. "Do you have any more witnesses?"

The prosecutor looked flustered. "I had one more, Kym Syndako, but she has failed to appear at this time. The prosecution reserves the right to call her to the stand when she arrives."

The judge looks at Mark. "Do you have any further witnesses that you'd like to call to the stand?"

"Yes, Your Honor," Mark replied. "I'd like to call Jenna Lewis to the stand at this time."

Jenna could hear murmurs from behind her. She looked straight ahead and walked shakily towards the witness box. She kept her eyes focused on Mark just as he had instructed her to.

"Miss Lewis," Mark began. "Can you please tell us in your own words what happened on the night of March twenty-fifth, 2016?"

Jenna explained the events of the night to the best of her knowledge. "Do you remember going to Mickey's Hideout that night?"

"Yes," Jenna replied.

"Do you recall drinking excessively that evening?"

"Yes, I do," Jenna responded.

"Did you encourage Allie, Cara, and Kym to leave the establishment?"

"Yes, I did. We all drank too much that night and I felt it best that we leave rather than continue drinking."

"What were the girls' responses when you asked them to leave?"

"Cara reluctantly agreed, Kym helped to gather our things, and Allie... " Jenna paused as she remembered Allie cozied up with Jeff in a booth kissing. She could feel the jealousy that had flared up that night.

"Miss Lewis, can you finish answering the question please?"

"I'm sorry," Jenna looked over at Allie. "Allie declined to leave and stayed at the bar instead."

"Do you have any recollection of driving the car upon leaving the establishment?" Mark asked.

"No, I don't," Jenna replied looking straight at the jury.

"No further questions, Your Honor," Mark stated and walked back to his table.

The prosecutor stood up and walked towards Jenna.

"Miss Lewis, let's go back to your testimony about Cara Donnelly driving erratically. Can you please clarify exactly what happened during that part of the evening?"

Jenna cleared her throat. "Cara was very upset about Trent Miller's infidelity. When we reached the car, Cara had the keys in her hand. I told her I would drive because she was so upset. Cara had stated that she had puked and was sober and then started the car. I had to jump into the passenger seat as the car started backing out of the driveway."

"If Cara had the keys then how did you acquire them?" the prosecutor asked.

"Cara had begun to feel sick again and pulled off to the side of the road to vomit. Once she was feeling better she apologized for driving so erratically and handed me the keys."

"Your friends are lucky to have someone so responsible," the prosecutor responded. "If you were so concerned about their wellbeing then why drive them to Mickey's Hideout? Why not take them home?"

"I wanted to, but then Allie had gotten a phone call from a friend asking her to meet him at Mickey's Hideout and she wanted to go."

Jenna was quiet for a minute and then said, "I'm not sure but I think Allie had taken the keys and drove us to Mickey's Hideout."

"So now you're changing your testimony?" the prosecutor asked quizzically.

Jenna looked at Mark confused. Mark started to stand up but before he could say anything the prosecutor continued, "So you went to another bar even though Cara was distraught and vomiting and Kym had lost her father that day is that correct?"

Jenna winced. "Yes," she said quietly.

"Please speak up Miss Lewis," the prosecutor demanded.

Jenna cleared her throat. Her heart was banging in her chest and she felt like she was having difficulty breathing. "Yes," she repeated.

"Miss Lewis, can you explain for the court why you were drinking so heavily once you arrived at Mickey's Hideout?"

Jenna could swear her heart stopped. "I don't remember."

The prosecutor smiled. "It seems like you remember most things from that night in vivid detail, so I'm surprised that you don't remember this. Luckily, I have a written statement from Kym Syndako that stated the reason you were drinking heavily is that you had a romantic interest in Allie Stratford's friend Jeff Parker. Is that accurate?"

Jenna's eyes flew to Allie's and she saw the shock and hurt on Allie's face. She looked down at her hands and then replied, "It was complicated. I would never hurt Allie and Jeff was leading me on. I was hurt and angry and confused."

The prosecutor continued, "So you drank."

Mark intervened. "Objection, Your Honor, leading the witness."

The prosecutor looked at the jury and smiled. "Your Honor, I'd like to introduce into evidence the surveillance tape from that evening. I would encourage the jury to observe the facial expression on Miss Lewis's face when she looks over at Miss Stratford and Mr. Parker."

A television appeared and soon Jenna was seen looking over towards Allie and Jeff. She was scowling, and she looked angry. She was seen ordering drinks and shots each time she looked at them.

Jenna wished she could disappear. She couldn't look at Allie. She couldn't look at Eric. She couldn't look at her parents who would surely have that expression of disappointment that she had seen so many times during her youth.

"No further questions, Your Honor. The prosecution rests."

The judge announced, "We'll commence tomorrow morning at eight a.m. to hear closing arguments."

Chapter 25
Closing Arguments

Jenna sat nervously at the table in front of the courtroom. The clock said 7:58 a.m. In two minutes closing arguments will begin and the fate of Jenna's life will be with the twelve jurors. In one way, Jenna was glad this nightmare was almost over but on the other hand she knew it would never be over. She would never have the closure of knowing if she truly was the driver or not. She will always live with the guilt that she might have been the one that killed her best friend.

The hands on the clock shifted to eight o'clock. A bailiff entered the courtroom. "Everyone rise for the Honorable Judge Wilcox."

The judge walked in and took his seat at the bench. "Everyone may be seated," announced the judge. "Today marks the end of testimony for Jenna Lewis. We will begin with closing arguments and then the jury will be charged with determining a verdict." Judge Wilcox looked over at the prosecutor. "Counselor, you may begin your closing argument.

Miss Thomason stood up and walked toward the jurors. "Ladies and gentlemen of the jury you have heard a lot of testimony during this trial. You have heard from several witnesses stating that Jenna Lewis had difficulty staying out of trouble with the law during her youth. You have heard from countless people testifying that Jenna was known as a party girl. Jenna was perceived as a rebellious child when she lived at home with her loving parents.

"You've heard from Jenna's doctor when he testified under oath that he told her each and every time that she had an obligation to refrain from mixing her medication with alcohol. Jenna was fully aware of the effects of mixing the two, yet she chose to do it anyway. The defense would like you to believe that Jenna was a responsible person who always put her friends' needs first, but I disagree. Jenna knowingly took that medication and drank excessively by her own volition. Jenna wasn't responsible, she was out of control.

"You will recall the surveillance tape from Mickey's Hideout showing the resentful look of jealousy and her constant need for yet another drink. You also witnessed Jenna pulling the keys out of her pocket intending to drive the car that ended Cara Donnelly's life.

"You've heard testimony from experts that placed Jenna Lewis's body in the vicinity of where the driver of the vehicle would be after an ejection from the car.

"Was Cara Donnelly's death intentional? No. Could it have been prevented? Yes. If Jenna Lewis had not encouraged her friend to leave the bar and get into the car with her that night Cara would be with us today. Cara, whose life was dedicated to helping others, who brought joy to so many people, will no longer have that opportunity.

"I ask the jury for a verdict of guilty. Guilty of knowingly putting Cara's life in harm's way. Guilty of abusing medication and alcohol. Guilty of operating a vehicle under the influence of drugs and alcohol and guilty of second degree manslaughter in the death of Cara Donnelly."

The prosecutor stood silently looking at the jury and pointing at Jenna. Jenna tried to shrink down into her chair. She agreed with the prosecutor. If it weren't for her Cara would still be alive.

Mark stood up and walked towards the jury. "Ladies and gentlemen of the jury, the prosecution would like for you to believe that Jenna is at fault for the death of Cara Donnelly but let's review the evidence. Jenna had gone off to college like many recent high school graduates choose to do. While in college she turned her life around. Her grades were decent, she was making friends, and she had gotten medical help.

"The prosecution has to prove ***beyond a reasonable doubt*** that Jenna was driving that car on that fateful night. There hasn't been any proof. Yes, we have seen a video tape showing Jenna pulling out her keys from her purse and holding them in her hand, but who's to say that she didn't hand them to someone else before getting in the car? Jenna has never confessed to driving the vehicle. What the state has presented before you is nothing but circumstantial evidence not evidence that should convict Miss Lewis of... "

The door to the courtroom swung open and a police officer walked briskly down the aisle towards the judge. He was out of breath like he had been running. The bailiff stopped him before the officer could walk any further. The officer whispered something in the bailiff's ear and handed him a large manila envelope. The bailiff nodded as the officer turned to start walking away. The judge banged the gavel and said, "You are interrupting court proceedings Officer Lawrence. Would you like to be charged with contempt of court?"

Officer Lawrence turned and faced the judge. "My apologies, Your Honor, but I have just received evidence pertinent to this case." John gave a meaningful glance at Eric.

The judge put on his glasses and looked at the bailiff. He looked skeptical but picked up his gavel and announced, "This court will take a recess until one o'clock. Counselors, I'd like to see both of you in my chambers."

Mark looked at the judge in disbelief. "Your Honor, I was in the process of delivering my closing statement. Is this really necessary?"

The judge looked at Mark warningly. "Counselor, I do not know if it's necessary or not, but the jury will be privy to all evidence in this case and if they are not then how can they in good conscience make a fair and impartial verdict? If you are going to question the way I run my courtroom I'd be happy to charge you with contempt of court."

"No, Your Honor," Mark replied clearly frustrated. "I am not questioning how you run your courtroom." He looked at Jenna and his expression looked grim. "May I have permission to confer with my client before meeting in your chambers, Your Honor?"

"Permission granted, counselor. We will all meet in my chambers thirty minutes from now after I have had a chance to see what this is about."

Mark motioned for Jenna to stand up and he led her to one of the many conference rooms in the courtroom. Mark didn't look happy. He looked at Jenna. "Is there something, *anything*, you haven't told me? I don't like surprises, Jenna."

Jenna looked dumbfounded. "No, nothing. I've told you everything, at least everything that I can remember."

Mark looked at her intently and let out a deep breath. "Okay then. I guess we're about to find out." He opened the door and motioned for her family to come in. God, he hated surprises.

There was a brief knock on the door and the bailiff entered and retrieved Mark. Jenna sat nervously on a chair as her parents spoke quietly in the corner. Her mom spoke up first, "Jenna, honey, don't worry. Mark is doing a great job. Everything will be okay."

Tears slowly started rolling down Jenna's face. She didn't reply. The stress of this trial, of rehashing every mistake she had ever made, had taken its toll. She was a disappointment. How could she not be?

Jenna took a deep breath and stood up. She wiped away her tears and hugged first her mom and then her dad. "You're right everything is going to be okay. I love both of you and thank you for being by my side every step of the way. I should probably clean myself up before Mark gets back. I don't want everyone to see what a mess I am."

Jenna knocked on the door and the bailiff opened it. "May I use the restroom?" she asked. He escorted her to a private restroom and stood outside the door. She turned on the cold water in the sink and cupped her hands underneath it. The splash of cold water felt refreshing. She reached for a paper towel to dry her face and noticed that a piece of the mirror was cracked in the corner. She looked at for a long time and then pried it out. It came out easily, it felt like fate. She held the piece of glass in her hand and sat on the floor. She could end this whole entire nightmare with a single stroke. She would no longer disappoint those she loved, and she refused to be a burden to anyone any more.

She held the glass shard tightly and slid it across her wrist. It felt less painful than her life at that moment. She watched as the blood began to flow out of her. She leaned against the wall and closed her eyes as darkness slowly began to descend upon her.

Chapter 26
The Verdict

Mark and the prosecutor sat across from the judge in his chambers. Judge Wilcox looked at both of them. "I have in front of me new evidence that was given to me by Officer Lawrence. It appears to be a written confession from Kym Syndako. He handed them each a copy of the confession and allowed them time to read it.

The prosecutor was the first to speak. "So she lied when she gave her statement to the police." The prosecutor said with frustration as she dropped the confession back onto the judge's desk.

"It appears to be that way," replied Judge Wilcox.

"Why is she changing her statement now?" Mark asked rereading the confession.

Judge Wilcox took off his glasses and rubbed his eyes. "I asked Officer Lawrence that same question. He replied that he wanted to be thorough in the investigation and decided it would be beneficial to question Miss Syndako again. He learned that she had flown back to China and when she didn't fly back on the ticket he sent her, he flew out to find her. He met with her mother, Mrs. Syndako, who handed him this confession."

"How do we know the confession is Kym's?" Miss Thomason asked skeptically.

Judge Wilcox leaned back in his chair. "Officer Lawrence had that same question, so he had a handwriting expert confirm that the confession is legitimate."

"Where is Kym Syndako now? She was supposed to be here testifying," the prosecutor said indignantly.

The judge let out a sigh. "Miss Thomason, not everything is black and white, and the reality is that sometimes there are extenuating circumstances. I have checked with a detective in China as well as Mrs. Syndako and her lawyer. They all corroborate the evidence. As far as this case is concerned Jenna did not commit this crime therefore..."

"My client is acquitted," Mark interrupted.

"Yes, Mr. Davis that is correct," the judge replied. "Do either of you have any further questions about this case before we return to the courtroom?" Judge Wilcox asked looking at them pointedly.

"No, Your Honor," Mark said grinning.

Miss Thomason stood up and placed the confession in her briefcase. "Congratulations, counselor," she said to Mark reaching out to shake his hand. "Maybe I'll see you again when we have our day in court with Miss Syndako."

Mark walked back towards the conference room to retrieve Jenna. He thought about Kym and wondered what finally made her confess. Probably guilt, he surmised. Whatever the case may be, he was glad. You can never predict how a jury will decide. As he walked towards the conference room he saw a flurry of medics in the hallway. Right before he reached the conference room he was stopped by a paramedic.

"I'm sorry sir but this hallway is closed," stated the medic.

Mark rolled his eyes. "My client is in that conference room," he said pointing to a room about five feet down the hall from them. The door was still closed which meant that the person needing medical attention couldn't be his client. "We are in the middle of a trial. I only need to get to my client and get her back to the court..." Mark stopped mid-sentence as he saw Jenna being wheeled out of the women's restroom.

She was surrounded by paramedics yelling, "Her BP is dropping! Dammit move faster! We don't have much time! We're losing her!"

Jenna, lying lifeless on a gurney, was rapidly being whisked down the hallway to an ambulance waiting to transport her to the hospital.

"What happened?" Mark asked incredulously.

Jenna's parents were already following Jenna down the hallway as the bailiff stood next to Mark watching and replied, "Attempted suicide. Guess she thought it was easier to end it than to serve her time."

Mark looked at him angrily and growled, "She was innocent."

Epilogue

It's been two years, and Jenna was just as nervous now as she was the first time she had done this. She heard her name being announced and she took a deep breath as walked onto the stage of McClellan University. She looked at all the innocent and maybe not so innocent faces. Faces of students who chose to be here and others who were forced to attend thanks to their professor. The auditorium grew dimmer except for the spotlight on Jenna. It was then that she told her story as she had a dozen times before.

When she was finished she always took questions and by now she knew what was coming. A girl of about nineteen stood in front of a microphone located on the floor. She reminded Jenna of herself at that age. "Why did Kym Syndako lie?"

Jenna smiled sadly at the young girl and said, "I have a letter I'd like to read. It's from Kym Syndako." She pulled out the envelope that she carried in her purse when coming to talk to college kids. She took out the paper and began to read aloud:

"Dear Jenna,

I know you must hate me for what I put you through, but I'd like to explain and maybe one day you will forgive me. I was the one who drove the car that night, not you. I thought I was sober and I knew that you were in no shape to drive. I made you hand me the keys before we got in the car. You were sitting behind me and it wasn't long before you were passed out in the back seat. Cara and I were talking, and it started raining very hard. I saw something jump out in front of the car and swerved to keep from hitting it. That's when the car flipped, and we were thrown from the car. When I came to I heard someone groaning from the car. I tried to drag myself over to help but I passed out again and didn't regain consciousness until I was at the hospital.

"I honestly thought the police would say it was just an accident. I never dreamed they would charge you with Cara's death. I told them that you were driving because I knew they would revoke my visa and send me back to China. I am so sorry this has happened. I know it is my fault and this is my way of fixing it. You and Cara and Allie are my sisters and I will miss all of you so much. Please know that I never wanted to hurt anyone. You have given me so much and I will forever be indebted to you. Thank you for your friendship and for allowing me to be a part of a family when mine was so far away.

"I want you to know that as you read this letter I am finally at peace. I am who I am, a girl who made a wrong choice and is trying to fix her mistake. So, although I may no longer be among the living, I will be watching over all of you and smiling with love and gratitude.

With Much Love,

Kym"

There was silence in the room and Jenna could hear a few sniffles from the audience. She had read this letter so many times that she could recite it from memory. She was silent for a minute as she let the power of her story sink in. She wished Kym were here so that she could say that she forgave her and that mistakes happen. She would tell her that there were other ways to fix mistakes, which she could attest to herself as she ran her finger over the scar that served as a reminder on her wrist. It's ironic but in a way, she felt like she and Kym were in this together. They both took a horrible situation and hoped to make a positive impact for others and that offered some comfort. Jenna took a few more questions and then it was over.

She walked backstage and smiled as she saw her husband holding their young daughter. He smiled back at Jenna and wrapped his arm around her holding her tight. Like every time before he whispered in her ear, "You may have saved a life today."

Jenna whispered back, "I hope so."

They walked out of the university hand in hand as her daughter babbled happily in her father's arms. It was a beautiful sunny day and the sky was dotted with white billowing clouds floating overhead. It was hard to believe another fall semester had already started. A young college student stopped her as she was walking down the stairs.

"Thank you for telling your story. It couldn't have been easy. I just want you to know that your story really touched me. I don't want to go into details, but I just wanted to say thank you."

Jenna was about to respond but heard her name being called. She turned her head and looked down the stairs. Allie was standing at the bottom of the steps watching her and looking nervous. Jenna stood in stunned silence. Eric looked at Jenna quizzically and followed her eyes to see a young woman with curly brown hair staring back at Jenna.

Jenna took a deep breath and turned back towards Eric. She gazed into his concerned eyes. "I'll catch up with you in a minute?"

He leant over and kissed her cheek. "Take your time we're not going anywhere."

Jenna watched Eric as he crossed the street and walked towards a huge shade tree and then she turned and looked back at Allie.

It wasn't a dream, Allie was still standing there. They stared at each other for a moment and then Allie smiled and shrugged. Jenna walked shakily down to her not quite sure what to say. They stood and stared at each other in silence then Allie blurted out nervously, "I'm sorry. I wanted to tell you that so many times, but I wasn't allowed to contact you. I miss you, I miss Cara, hell I even miss Kym. I miss the way we were. I miss us." Allie tried to wipe away the tears that continued to fall.

Jenna smiled at Allie and realized that what Allie said was exactly how she felt. Since the accident, it was as if a huge black cloud hovered above her, sucking the life out of her until now. Jenna's eyes filled with tears and she quickly wiped them away as she looked at her best friend. She pulled Allie towards her and hugged her tight then whispered, "I've missed you too."

A vehicle honked from the road and both women turned their heads. An old, rusty, blue Volkswagen Van with paint peeling along the sides had stopped on the road in front of them. There was a red canoe strapped tightly to the top. Jenna's eyes traveled down toward the driver and she was shocked to see Jeff waving from the window. "Are you...?" she asks Allie bewildered.

Allie laughed and nodded. "Yes, we're officially together. In fact," she held up her left hand, "We just got married and we are about to leave on our honeymoon. We are going away for a month and driving across the country. Life's too short, you know?"

"Wow!" replied Jenna. "Congratulations! I didn't see that coming but you two have always been destined to be together. Anyone could see that. I know you will both be very happy."

"We are," Allie replied. "Once we get back I'll be moving to Kensington where Jeff lives. We've already rented a house."

Jenna smiled and said, "I'm really happy for you Allie. I mean that. It's really good to see you."

Allie turned her head and motioned to the dark-haired man playing with a curly haired little girl under the shade tree. She raised her eyebrow with a twinkle in her eye. "A family?" she asked teasingly. "It seems I'm not the only one who's getting their life on track."

Jenna chortled, "Yeah, I'm pretty lucky. I have an amazing husband and the most adorable daughter. I'm very lucky."

Allie didn't let up. "And how did you meet this amazing husband of yours?"

Jenna laughed and said, "He was the one who arrested me."

Allie shook her head laughing. "If I wasn't already married I'd say he could handcuff me anytime."

Both girls laughed, and Jeff honked again motioning to Allie that it was time to go. Allie leant over and gave Jenna one last hug before heading towards the car. "I love you, Jenna," she whispered.

"I love you too, Allie," Jenna replied, hugging her tight.

Jenna walked over to where Eric and Nellie were playing. "Are you okay?" Eric asked looking concerned.

She snuggled into his arms and smiled. "Better than okay." She picked up Nellie and smothered her with kisses then leant into Eric feeling his arms wrap around her. "Let's go home."